One Simple Favor

J. L. Salter

δ
Dingbat Publishing

Because my son is the soul of kindness (and always doing favors for others), I dedicate this novella to David Jeffrey Salter.

Prologue

Sunday, 10:12 p.m.

My stomach grumbled as I exited the gas station's restroom. I considered purchasing a candy bar, but then figured Aunt Mary would have ready a hearty stew or some other dish she could easily keep warm. So instead my next stop was the coffee machine, not far from a loud argument between a hostile man and a crying woman. But I tuned it out—plenty of travelers bicker when they're stressed from the road.

Then, out of the corner of my eye, I noticed Mike intently studying the entire scene.

Suddenly the angry man whacked the woman with a backhand. She yelped and added a combination of cursing and pleading to her sobs. Before I'd finished pouring my coffee, the man was roughing her up even more—shoving and yelling.

Being in the middle of a public nocturnal domestic dispute was the last thing I wanted, so I tried to signal Mike it was time to leave. But he'd moved from his former spot near the overpriced chips and stood about four feet from angry, violent Fisty and his cringing, crying girlfriend.

I even tried waving, but nothing I did registered at all—Mike's complete attention was on the aggressive brute. I figured my cousin-in-law was about two seconds from getting clobbered himself.

Then I heard Mike. Not the actual words initially—just his strong, firm, authoritative voice speaking to the man.

Whatever Mike said evidently got the attacker's attention, because Fisty dropped the woman like a limp blanket and whipped around. "What'd ya say?"

"I said leave her alone... back away. This isn't the time or place... or the proper handling of whatever's bothering you."

"You want me to show ya some proper handling?" asked Fisty. And he unleashed a haymaker that would've decked Muhammed Ali.

With a blur of sidestep and arm motion, Mike deflected that blow and instantly kung fu'd a maneuver that put the creep face down on the floor, with his arm twisted high behind his back and Mike's knee pressed sharply between his shoulders.

I dropped my coffee.

Scalding liquid splashing to the floor barely registered, because I was in shock. I'd need super slow mo and a rewind button to figure out all of Mike's moves, but my heart pounded and I thought I might faint. Hadn't felt that way since a live concert with Justin Timberlake...

1

Sunday, 9:10 p.m.

Hate getting roped into favors that get me off-route and off-schedule. I was already exhausted before even starting my drive home from Memphis, and the hectic rush-hour traffic west of Nashville was making me late. Some distant cousin finally appears after all these years for some whoopty-doo hunting trip and the only person who can make the bus station grab is me?

Just one more favor I owed Aunt Mary for all the sacrifices she'd made for me... most of which she remembered in such detail, they might have been written on a tablet next to her wall phone.

Of course, by the time I reached the crowded, dirty station at 9:20 and found a distant parking place, a bus had just pulled out. Didn't catch the destination on its big front sign, though I guessed it wouldn't matter much where it headed next. Obviously it was not traveling to Verdeville.

I hurried toward the entrance, still fuming. When I'd explained I couldn't predict when I'd reach the station, she'd said, "It's okay, dear, they have chairs, don't they?" To Auntie, life was simple like that—she remembered the 1950s as though they were yesterday.

When I'd asked what Cousin Michael looked like, she'd said, "Oh, I'm not sure, dear. Nobody's seen him since he was a schoolboy."

"Don't you have even a general idea of his appearance now?"

"In the only photo I could find," she said, "he's a skinny kid about eleven, in a saggy swimsuit at a beach. Big feet and dark hair."

"Gosh, he ought to be easy to find."

Either Auntie had no radar for sarcasm or (infuriatingly) she ignored it and replied, "How many Michaels could be on the same bus?"

I'd carefully entered his bus number and arrival time into my cell phone. But at a stop light, around 9:15 when I'd tried to let her know I was running late, my battery was stone cold dead. Didn't have my extra phone cord that charges from the car. Par for the course. How did I get stuck picking up cousin Michael what's-his-name? *What is his last name, anyway?*

"Michael Something, Michael Who's-It," I pondered. He was related through Aunt Mary, who'd married Cleve Nolan, my mom's only brother. But I couldn't recall ever hearing Auntie's maiden name!

Well, if I couldn't find some sort of Michael arriving from Missouri, I could call Auntie from the station. Or was it a different "M" state? Mississippi?

Impatiently, I joined the ticket window line and finally got to ask if the bus from Missouri had arrived. The rather snarly agent looked up from his computer and said, "Buses from Missouri arrive several times daily. What city is your party coming from?"

"Don't remember, but if I can use your phone, I'll ask Aunt Mary."

Mr. Snarl rifled through his paperwork basket and finally located the item he clearly wanted to shove in my face. "Terminal Employees are not 'allowed' to let Customers use our Phones." I could tell the sign was locally made because the caps were all wrong and the composer had used scare quotes.

Nonetheless, he had me buffaloed. "Well, just tell me which Missouri cities have sent buses here this evening."

Seemed like Mr. Snarl would burst a vein in his forehead. Instead of producing another sign, however, he glared and recited in a slow monotone, "Arrivals and departures are posted on the board." Wearily, and with his vein throbbing visibly, Mr. Snarl pointed. "Above that bank of TVs." Then, with a wave of his thin, hairy hand, he figuratively shoved me aside. "Next."

"You think you've gotten the last laugh, Mr. Snarl," I said to myself as I glared back. "But I'm going to use you as a character in a story." Yes, I'm a writer. Expecting to be an author soon, but that depends partly on the mood of some intern sitting on the slush pile at any of the dozen literary agencies where I'd sent my second complete novel. I had shown my first manuscript to Aunt Mary—which evidently had added significantly to how many favors I now owed her. After reading it, she'd kissed my cheek and said, "I know your next one will be better, dear."

Standing in front of the televisions, I noted one did not work at all and another displayed little more than electronic snow. According to the third screen, whatever buses scheduled to arrive around 8:50 had already come and gone and now the only routes showing from any Missouri cities would be arriving hours later. I looked for other states that started with "M". Only one listing for Michigan, but who travels from there?

The single pay phone, off in a dingy corner, had an *Out of "Order"* sign on it. Even that forlorn sign had scare quotes.

Considered asking a stranger to loan me a phone, but none of the faces looked friendly enough—or safe enough—to engage. As Aunt Mary would intone, "That would be uncautious, dear." In fact, at least two individuals looked like movie axe murderers—desperate and grungy, with dull eyes.

Presumably Cousin Michael—likely disgruntled by his wait—was still there somewhere. Eliminating fully half of the travelers by gender, I could ignore at least half of the males because of evident age, though I quickly realized it's more difficult to guess the ages of tired bus travelers.

That left five males who could conceivably be within a few years of Michael's late twenties. When I began staring at my first suspect, he went towards the men's room, so I figured I'd better come up with a better strategy than the ones they use on TV.

Rummaging in my purse, I found a small note tablet. *Wish I'd written the bus info there instead of tapping it into my phone.* I turned the tablet sideways and wrote, "Michael? Verdeville?"

Standing about seven feet away from one suspect, I got his attention and raised my sign. He smiled lasciviously and placed one hand on his crotch. Nope, wrong cousin.

Backing away, I perched as close to the main door as

possible and tried to hatch a different plot. "If you ever find this guy," I said to myself, "this wipes the slate clean of favors you owe Auntie." I hated being off-course and out of my familiar scheduling. *Life is difficult enough when you color inside the lines.*

No two ways about it, I had to let Aunt Mary know I'd probably missed Michael. But I was stymied unless I could access a working phone, so I dragged myself out of the terminal's hard plastic seat, which I just then discovered had a film of partly dried beverage—hopefully not something more offensive—all over it. *Now it's likely on the butt of my jeans, too.*

As if telepathically aware of my dilemma, an older lady with weathered dark skin caught my eye and motioned me closer. When I warily got within about six feet, she whispered, "Are you in trouble, young lady?"

"Not really trouble, but I sure could use your phone, if you wouldn't mind."

Reaching into her purse, she held up her phone. "One call, if you promise to keep it short and swear you won't call one of those overseas scammers."

"No, ma'am, it's just to my aunt in the next county over."

"Very well, but keep it short. My bus leaves soon." She lifted her glasses to examine the device and then pressed two buttons. "It's ready for your number."

"Thank you, ma'am. This is a lifesaver." It was a miracle I could even remember Aunt Mary's home number.

Auntie's phone rang nine times before anyone answered. Just my luck to get the hard-of-hearing uncle who never talked on the phone.

"Uncle Cleve? It's Tricia. I'm still in Nashville. Haven't

found Cousin Michael and I'm afraid I might've missed him somehow. Can you tell me which city he came from and remind me of his last name?"

My uncle had one of his coughing fits. When Cleve finally settled back down, he asked me to start over.

"Can I just talk to Aunt Mary?" After I restated that question a few times, he said she was at the neighbor's house helping fix a "mess" with a quilting pattern. *I've got my own mess right here.* So I patiently repeated all my questions, as the kindly depot passenger monitored me closely.

"Missed him?" asked Uncle Cleve. So he'd heard at least some of my context, though he didn't help with any of my queries except to confirm the scheduled arrival time of 8:50 — some forty minutes ago.

When the loudspeaker abruptly announced a departure, the kind lady stood and reached for her phone. I hurriedly asked Uncle Cleve again for Michael's last name and origination point, but he started coughing once more. The lady grabbed her phone and hustled toward the exit.

Rats. I'd had one decent phone chance and wasted it on deaf Uncle Cleve.

What now? Outside the terminal in the gloomy dark, I looked all directions for the nearest place which might have a working pay phone. Spotting no prospects, I just groaned and headed toward the parking lot.

I was still near the main terminal entrance when I saw a young guy wearing a ball cap, possibly late twenties, standing next to a duffle bag and extending his thumb to the occasional cars cruising along the drop off / pick up lane.

Approaching, but not getting too close, I attracted his attention with an enthusiastic wave and held up my tablet.

When he grinned in a puzzled sort of way, I realized I'd

shown him the cardboard backing, so I hurriedly flipped back over to the sign. In case he couldn't read, I verbalized the whole point: "Michael?"

To which he replied, "Yeah, Mike."

Michael, Mike, whatever. "Headed to Verdeville?"

He answered slowly. "Suurrre."

What a relief I'd finally found him, but suddenly a wave of shyness hit me. I didn't figure to hug a distant in-law I'd never met, so I just extended my hand. When he held it in a firm grasp, it warmed me down to my toes. Then he searched my eyes as though he were also calculating our exact familial tie.

In truth, he was not actually my cousin, so it was time to come clean. "You're a grandson of my Aunt Mary's first cousin."

He squinted as though the calculation hurt. "Possibly so."

Seemed a bit spacey to me. Had he not looked so fit, I would've wondered if he was one of those laid-back couch potatoes who played video games all day. "But we've never met because I don't know any of Auntie's family. They're all clustered in another state." I stuffed the tablet back into my purse. "So we're not really third cousins. I guess we'd be cousins-in-law, and removed at least twice."

"At least." Then his eyes widened. "Yeah, I think I re-member an Aunt Mary... somewhere." When he pointed, his biceps clarified he was no couch potato.

My pulse stuttered, making me wary. "You *were* expect-ing me, weren't you?"

"Wasn't expecting anyone in particular, but I'm pleased to meet you, uh, cousin."

"Tricia. Sorry. Tricia Pilgrim."

"No problem, I'm easy."

Yes, he was. Easy going but chiseled hard. "My car's over there somewhere." I pointed vaguely toward the distant gloom of the parking lot.

"Okay."

"Thank goodness I finally found you." For a third cousin-in-law, removed at least twice, he was kind of cute. "So I guess we should get going."

He shrugged into the denim jacket lying atop his duffle. "Cool."

2

9:40 p.m.

H-Hour was 9 a.m. on Monday, when I had to return to work a day early and face a vital, unscheduled half-day session. I was supposed to have Monday off as my floating holiday but the boss had called Friday evening after I'd already reached Memphis and announced he'd just been notified of a surprise audit. Fortunately, a friend up the line had discreetly and unofficially alerted him. The reason I had to be there was because Mr. Dross hardly ever looked at his own accounting company's books and left them totally to me, the office manager, not yet finished with my coursework for the CPA exam. So I was additionally nervous that any tiny glitch those corporate suits might find in the office records would somehow reflect poorly on my efforts to secure CPA accreditation.

I was pretty certain it was illegal for a supervisor to cancel a floating holiday after it had been approved, but if I wanted to keep my job I'd have to appear anyway... and haggle over the expropriated holiday later.

I couldn't stifle my exhausted yawn. The first half of my weekend in Memphis had been a fiasco anyway. Missed connections, missed opportunities, missed everything... might as well cut it short.

En route to the car with my distant cousin-in-law, I still grumbled to myself. I could only hope to drop him off and be home by 10:30 p.m., so I'd still have a reasonably normal night to rest up before the audit and all the stress from Mr. Dross looking over my shoulder and telling me to hurry.

Cousin Mike wasn't particularly talkative, so I watched his face for visual clues about what he was thinking. Of course, the sidewalk was so dark it was difficult to see much except his general features—a strong chin, handsome brow. I didn't want to be too obvious, but several furtive glances revealed he was tallish—about six foot one—nice shoulders, apparently trim waist. With his boots and jeans and faded denim jacket, he could've been anything from a cowboy to an oilfield roughneck. Or just a casual dresser.

I hadn't noticed when I'd hurriedly parked, but the gateway to the lot had a heavy bank of dark bushes on each side. As we were about to enter, Mike did a curious thing— he clutched my arm and held me back until he'd poked his head around the corner and looked both ways. Then he released my arm and we proceeded.

"Expecting someone?"

"Not really." He shook his head. "But I usually want to know if anybody's on the other side of something before I stick my neck through it."

"Makes sense, I guess. Wouldn't want to be uncautious, as Auntie always says." I paused and strained to examine his expression. Too dark. "Well, that's me, over there." I pointed to the silverish Toyota sedan, about seven years old and well over 100,000 miles. It took only a few more seconds to reach it. "Just toss that in the back."

Instead of tossing, he carefully placed his duffle bag in the rear and then seated himself in the front passenger seat. I backed from the slot and headed out of the lot toward I-24, which would take us to the I-440 loop and eventually to I-40 East.

Not wanting to admit I'd forgotten it, I fished around for cousin Mike's last name. "You know, it's funny how Auntie refers to my uncle's Nolan relatives as *his* nephews and nieces or *his* cousins rather than *their* nephews and nieces or cousins."

"And when a cousin's mother's married name is different, it's like you're not only an in-law, but an entirely different family altogether." Mike smiled wryly.

"Completely different," I said, as I tried to calculate whether he'd stated it correctly.

"Of course, in some families, the in-law status makes little or no difference, but in other families, it's a high, solid wall of delineation."

I'd misjudged Mike by thinking him spacey—he had an alert mind and impressive vocabulary. "Especially if your uncle's Nolan side has hardly ever even seen your aunt's side."

Mike faced me. "Yeah. Just like I've never heard of your clan—the Pilgrims."

"Well, that's logical because my mom, a Nolan, married my dad, a Pilgrim. Aunt Mary's a Nolan now, since she married my mom's brother. So you pretty much think of yourself as Michael…"

"Mike, actually. But I don't mind Michael." He still

didn't supply his surname, but nodded as he held on to the conversational thread. "I'm aware of my mom's ancestry, of course."

Of course.

"Though I fully realize half of my bloodline comes through my mom's side, I think I sense my identity lies with my father's name, Stagg."

Also logical I wouldn't have heard of *his* mom's married name.

He shrugged. "So we're like total strangers, you and me."

Indeed. "That's one reason, I think, that Auntie wanted me to pick you up... so our different family groups could finally make some cross-family contact."

"I'm game."

I checked a highway sign. "You know, Mike, it occurs to me that if our discussion were dialog in a stage play, the audience would suspect that we were talking about two completely different families." The road was briefly clear so I eyed him quickly. "You follow me?"

Mike became more animated and faced me in the dark car. "I was just thinking the same thing. A lot of great literature has that kind of theme... lookalikes, disguises, and other mistakes often take the characters on a wild ride."

I guess my fatigue made me laugh louder than I normally would've.

Mike monitored my face... and apparently checked out my bosom while he was in the neighborhood. Unfortunately, I was dressed for driving, not to impress cousins— flats with straps, nice-fitting jeans, and a buttoned cotton blouse. A sweater in the back seat.

"Speaking of rides, how far is it?"

"To Verdeville? About thirty miles or so. After we finally clear the eastern loop of Nashville, it's clear sailing on I-40."

"Big place?"

I chuckled. "How long since you visited Verdeville, Mike?"

"Don't recall ever."

"Oh, that's weird. Auntie seemed to suggest that photo was taken in Verdeville."

"What photo?"

"You at Lake Envie. Or at *some* lake, anyhow."

"Must've been a different lake."

"Guess so." I pointed toward the radio. "You want any music?"

"Not particularly, but I don't mind if you need it."

Didn't *need* it—was just trying to be polite. I must have sighed because he looked my way again. "Sometimes silence is the prettiest music."

Maybe so. And his peculiarly astute observation gave me a warm tingle.

Mike leaned back in his seat and adjusted the visor of his cap.

"Want to take a quick snooze?" I asked. "Power nap before we arrive?"

"Actually, I'd rather get some coffee, if you wouldn't mind stopping somewhere. From the look and smell of the stuff in that bus station, I think they use it to kill mutant roaches."

Ugh. "You read my mind. I was craving caffeine also." I pointed vaguely east. "There's an exit right after we clear the loop."

"Cool."

"By the way, I'm sorry I was late back there. But I lost the route number, arrival time, et cetera. Everything was in my phone and the stinking battery died again."

"Happens. I don't even carry a phone." He gazed out the window again. "No problem. Like I said, I wasn't expecting anyone in particular to pick me up."

"If it'd been *me* stranded at the Nashville bus station at night, I think I'd have freaked."

"I guess I've done my share of that, too, but it doesn't usually help the situation or circumstances." He faced me lazily. "So I try to keep reasonably calm and tolerably mellow."

I vaguely wondered *why* he was so mellow—or was he merely distracted?—but that's not the kind of thing you ask a distant cousin you just met. "We've only got another mile or two on the loop before we turn east and hit that coffee exit."

Still quite placid, he nodded.

"So, I guess you're really looking forward to this big hunting thing they've planned."

His eyebrows went up. "Hadn't heard anything about it."

"I thought that was one of the main reasons you were visiting."

"Nope. In fact, I was actually touring this area more than visiting any particular place."

"Huh?"

"Besides, I don't have a hunting license in Tennessee."

"I guess they've rigged up a visitor permit or something."

"Maybe so." Then Mike went into some detailed perspective about various animal species and how interesting it was that some lived at different altitudes and climates exclusively. I couldn't follow too closely because I had to keep my focus on the multi-lane traffic and didn't dare miss the ramp off the loop to I-40 east. I picked up enough phrases, however, to conclude that Mike didn't sound like he'd planned to spend Monday and possibly Tuesday in the woods.

"Well, I'm sure Auntie has everything worked out."

No particular reaction from the cousin, but he seemed to soak it all in, like the dark scenery and occasional lights zooming past his window at 67 mph.

But I was still trying to make it all fit together. "I'll bet you'll be borrowing one of Uncle Cleve's guns."

"Possibly so." Sounded as if Mike were following a detective show on TV rather than settling a question about his own arrangements. "I'm easy."

Yes, you are, Mike. Very easy. "As matter of fact, you seem quite relaxed."

"Well, that wasn't always the case. I used to be pretty tense at times. But here in the past few months, I guess I've had a make-over of sorts."

I nodded sympathetically. Aunt Mary had told me about his dad dying a few years back, Michael's aimlessness after a nasty break-up, and his mom's worries about him. "I understand. Auntie said you could use a role model or mentor."

He looked puzzled again. "Well, there are plenty of great role models in the movies, as far as I'm concerned."

"From movies?"

"Sure. Take *Die Hard*, for example. That detective just goes to the big party to hook up with his estranged wife, but he ends up being the one everybody's counting on. And he doesn't let them down."

I remembered the movie well enough, but didn't see any connection with Aunt Mary's description of Michael's life. "Not sure Auntie's seen that film."

"You ought to rent it and show her… it's a classic."

As I tried to picture Aunt Mary watching Bruce Willis wipe out a whole squad of bad guys, Mike tapped my elbow and pointed. "There… gas station on the right. They'll have coffee."

"And a restroom, I hope." *I dared not even peek in the one at the bus station.* I pulled in and parked at the front.

3

10:12 p.m.

My stomach grumbled as I exited the gas station's restroom. I considered purchasing a candy bar, but then figured Aunt Mary would have ready a hearty stew or some other dish she could easily keep warm. So instead my next stop was the coffee machine, not far from a loud argument between a hostile man and a crying woman. But I tuned it out—plenty of travelers bicker when they're stressed from the road.

Then, out of the corner of my eye, I noticed Mike intently studying the entire scene.

Suddenly the angry man whacked the woman with a backhand. She yelped and added a combination of cursing and pleading to her sobs. Before I'd finished pouring my coffee, the man was roughing her up even more—shoving and yelling.

Being in the middle of a public nocturnal domestic dispute was the last thing I wanted, so I tried to signal Mike it was time to leave. But he'd moved from his former spot near the overpriced chips and stood about four feet from angry, violent Fisty and his cringing, crying girlfriend.

I even tried waving, but nothing I did registered at all — Mike's complete attention was on the aggressive brute. I figured my cousin-in-law was about two seconds from getting clobbered himself.

Then I heard Mike. Not the actual words initially—just his strong, firm, authoritative voice speaking to the man.

Whatever Mike said evidently got the attacker's attention, because Fisty dropped the woman like a limp blanket and whipped around. "What'd ya say?"

"I said leave her alone... back away. This isn't the time or place... or the proper handling of whatever's bothering you."

"You want me to show ya some proper handling?" asked Fisty. And he unleashed a haymaker that would've decked Muhammed Ali.

With a blur of sidestep and arm motion, Mike deflected that blow and instantly kung fu'd a maneuver that put the creep face down on the floor, with his arm twisted high behind his back and Mike's knee pressed sharply between his shoulders.

I dropped my coffee.

Scalding liquid splashing to the floor barely registered, because I was in shock. I'd need super slow mo and a rewind button to figure out all of Mike's moves, but my heart pounded and I thought I might faint. Hadn't felt that way since a live concert with Justin Timberlake.

"What on earth?" I approached tentatively while the counter clerk called somebody on his phone—probably the police. The woman was still sobbing, so I found myself heading her direction, though unsure what I'd do or say to an abused stranger.

The thug on the floor thrashed a bit until Mike tightened his arm lock, applied more knee pressure, and ended all resistance. "Now are you ready to settle down, dude?"

His muffled response was clearly rage mixed with pain.

"Guess not." Mike removed Fisty's loose belt and used it to bind the bad guy's hands behind his back. To the clerk, Mike said, "Better leave him tied up 'til the cops get here."

The wide-eyed employee nodded, apparently with as much additional adrenaline as I felt coursing through myself.

"What just happened, Mike?" My whisper came out as a frightened hiss.

"We couldn't let him beat up a defenseless woman."

Why'd he say "we"? "I don't mean the mugging, I mean what you're doing."

"This wasn't a mugging… it was domestic."

"And you're deliberately avoiding my point."

"We can discuss it later." He nodded toward the spill. "Right now, get three coffees and let's go."

"Three?" I did a double-take at the woman still struggling to rise from the floor. I'd started in her direction but never made it. "No way. The clerk can take care of her."

"No, he won't. He didn't lift a finger to help her a minute ago." He lowered his voice. "She needs assistance and safe harbor."

"Just tell the clerk to call a shelter. He'll listen to you."

Mike eyed the man behind the counter and shook his head slowly. "Only as long as I'm here, but not after I leave."

I couldn't guess how he'd discerned that. "So what happens?"

"You've got room in your car for one more rider."

"Are you nuts?"

"I don't see the problem. Just shift a few things to the trunk."

We both watched the victim stand and straighten her jeans and t-shirt. "Mike, I can't be responsible for her safety."

"You aren't."

"If she's in my car, I will be."

"I'll take responsibility. She can't stay here."

"Why not?" I hissed. "The police can get her to a shelter."

Mike held up one hand in the international signal for *hang on a minute.* "Go get some paper towels." Then he went to the woman and spoke softly, briefly.

Securing towels from the reluctant clerk, I returned and handed most of them to the woman. She had a bloody nose and cut lip. Plus abrasions. And the look in her eyes held more fear than I'd ever seen before. Thirty seconds ago, I'd wanted to flee the scene, but now I felt like beating that bully senseless. Wasn't sure where such rage came from. Fortunately for both of us, Mike had already neutralized him.

"Shondell only needs a ride to her grandmother's house… just up the road a bit."

He already knew her name. For some reason, that made me feel vaguely ashamed. "How far?"

"Sounded close."

Angry or not, I still didn't want to get involved any more than we already were. *Off my schedule, off my course.* "Mike, this is nuts." Then I whispered. "She's a total stranger. We don't know…"

"If you were the one battered, would it be nuts for somebody to drive you to safety?"

I've always hated it when logical truth trumps my raw

emotional fears. All I could do was shrug... with an extra shiver. "One quick ride to Grannie's and then I'm done."

"Come on, Shondell," he said, extending his hand. "We've got room for you."

"You sure?" Shondell regarded Mike through her tears and didn't even acknowledge my presence. "Thanks."

I tossed my remaining paper towel over the spill, grabbed three fresh coffees and a candy bar, and paid cash. The clerk begged me to stick around for the police report, but I just inclined my head toward Mike leading the woman out the door. "They're in my car."

"Hey, man!" yelled the clerk. "The cops are on their way, man."

Without pausing, Mike spoke over his shoulder. "We've got miles to go before we sleep, dude. Miles to go."

"You positive you wouldn't rather wait for the police?" I asked.

Mike's only reply: "Are you driving? Or me?"

"My car." I clutched the keys tighter.

He opened the trunk and carefully placed his duffle inside, then made sure Shondell was comfortable in the back seat. After a look over his shoulder, he got in front and pointed north, away from the interstate ramp.

We had hardly cleared the parking lot when the flashing lights of a police cruiser appeared over a half mile behind us. I was already another mile along Donelson Pike by the time the officers would have exited their vehicle and begun sizing up the situation at the gas station.

I tried to keep one eye on the road, one on my mirror to monitor Shondell in the back seat, and another on Mike. But I ran out of eyeballs.

Mike quietly confirmed something with Shondell, who

still had not spoken out loud to me, and then said, "Her grandmother lives in a community up this way."

"How far?"

"Just past a little bridge. She's not sure about the street name, but she'll recognize it when she sees it."

My belly frozen over, I fumbled with my Styrofoam cup and poured down some coffee to melt the ice. "Mike, this doesn't sound good to me."

"It'll be all right." We crossed the little bridge. Another brief, whispered conference with Shondell. "Take the next left."

I searched in vain for a street sign so I could get myself out of this area in case I ended up dumping both Shondell and Cousin Mike out here in the sticks. I also made a mental note—for after we got rid of this back-seat stranger—to ask Mike two things. One, how could someone that mellow turn so quickly into a ninja? And two, why had he been so eager to get moving?

Mike's tap on my shoulder interrupted my thoughts. "Next right. Little house between those two trailers."

I shuddered. No street lights. Not even any visible light in the windows of those three structures. "Are you sure?"

He nodded. "It's okay. Trust me."

Even though he was a wannabe ninja, he was asking a lot for me to trust a twice-removed third cousin-in-law whom I'd never seen before in my life. But I dutifully pulled in. A huge dog barked. "I think I'll stay in the car."

"Okay." Then he got out and helped Shondell from my Toyota to Grannie's front stoop.

I discreetly locked the car doors as I watched Mike explain things to Grannie, who—with tears streaming down her weathered face—hugged Shondell tightly. Then Mike pulled something from his pocket and pressed it into Grannie's hand. As he turned, but before he actually moved from the stoop, Grannie latched onto him, sobbing. I couldn't hear her words, but in such situations dialog is superfluous. Somehow I wished I could be in the middle of that impromptu group embrace.

Shortly Mike returned to my car. Before he got in, he tapped on the trunk lid, which I opened using the inside latch. He carefully retrieved his duffle and gently placed it back on the rear seat where it had been.

Wonder what's in that bag? My curiosity was thoroughly aroused but I didn't feel I knew him well enough yet to ask.

"See?" He got settled and fixed his seatbelt. "That didn't take long."

"Maybe not, but look where we are."

Mike's eyes took in the dismal panorama. "Nowhere in particular, but it's one more place I've never been."

"Mighty dark place, too." When I started the car, something smelled funny. *Must be somebody burning leaves or trash somewhere.* I headed back the way we'd come. "Oh, crud. I should've used her phone to call Auntie."

"Not sure she had one."

He was probably right. "So what was that you gave her?"

He shrugged. "She said they were short on groceries."

I made the turn south on Donelson Pike, toward the I-40 ramp, and tried to stay on the road as I studied Mike's face. Who or what was he? And where did chivalrous gentlemen like him come from? More importantly, how come I'd never met somebody like Mike who *wasn't* related to me?

He sensed my puzzlement. "Okay, things have settled down, Tricia. Which part confuses you the most?"

4

10:29 p.m.

As Mike explained—to his own satisfaction, anyway—why he'd gotten involved in Shondell's domestic dispute, all I could think was how it had disrupted my already distorted schedule. Yeah, I know that sounds selfish, but my life needs predictability and timetable—I can't allow side trips to throw me off kilter. Especially when I'm already exhausted, dreading Monday's surprise audit, fed up with the bizarre micro-management from my boss, and totally bummed out from the Memphis debacle.

This had been bothering me since I stood watching Mike take down Fisty—so I had to ask. "Mike, are you sure we're cousins?"

"You said so yourself."

"Yeah, but I don't recall Aunt Mary ever saying anything about you being a ninja fighter."

"That was just ordinary hand-to-hand. And besides, I don't actually remember your aunt, either."

"Wonder why?"

"Some families have squabbles or misunderstandings and go for many years with no contact. Maybe Aunt Mary got mad at somebody."

"Or somebody got mad at her."

"Either way. It wouldn't be a family if somebody's nose wasn't out of joint about something."

He was probably right.

Up ahead, the police cruiser's lights still flashed in the gas station parking lot. "Looks like it's taking them awhile to clear things up. Want to stop and help them out?"

"No." Sudden agitation. "In fact, let's not take that ramp after all."

"What do you mean?"

"Isn't there another highway around here that goes east?"

I sputtered. Nobody drove on the old highway any more except the folks who lived off its shoulders. "Well, Highway 70 meanders that direction, but it's a lot slower going."

"Can we get to 70 without passing that station?"

I nodded, but was troubled. "I need to ask you some-thing—cousin-in-law to third cousin-in-law twice removed."

"Shoot."

There was no traffic, so I slowed to nearly a crawl. "Is there any particular reason you'd prefer *not* to see police right now?" My eyes were mostly on the road but I could tell he was watching my face intently.

"How much truth can you handle this late, after what's been apparently a very tiring and confusing day for you?"

That wasn't an answer. "Mike, Highway 70 is north of the interstate. I believe we can reach it not far from where we turned off for Grannie's house." It was a different number until we reached the county line, but it became 70. "I'll only reverse course if you'll tell me why."

He craned his neck. "Get us on that other highway and I'll tell you whatever you want to know."

It was about four minutes before I reached Highway 24 and turned east. As Mike kept monitoring the passenger rear view mirror, I drove through the small town of Hermitage and stopped at what appeared to be the last business on that side of town. It was a hardware store, dark and closed. Switched off the engine, still smelling those burning leaves, and faced him. "Okay, what's this all about? Are you *wanted* anywhere?"

He grinned. Quite charming, in that dangerous sense of wait-'til-you-hear-my-explanation. "Would you believe me if I said I wasn't breaking the spirit of the law even though I'm technically bending the *letter*?"

"Somehow I can totally believe it."

"And would it make any difference to you if this, uh, breach had no selfish motive?"

My eyes rolled backward. "Don't tell me it's some Robin Hood scam."

"Not Robin Hood, but I do like that dude. He's another good role model."

"Whatever." I circled my hand forward.

"Okay, I'm carrying."

"Carrying what?"

"You know… grass."

I sputtered vowels and consonants, but without any discernable words.

"It's not for me." Mike clutched my wrist, refocusing my attention. "Besides, it's medicinal."

"So says everybody with a joint."

"This really is. I have a friend..."

More sputter. "It's always somebody holding for a friend."

"Do you want me to explain or not?" He sounded quite perturbed.

"Okay." I groaned as I stared toward the dark store and kept sniffing that odd rusty-smoky smell. Maybe it wasn't burning trash. *No time to worry about it now.* "Explain away."

"It's a guy I know in Knoxville. He's real sick. A veteran." Mike swallowed hard. "Ralph's in bad shape and can't seem to move up the VA waiting list to get any relief."

"You aren't doing him any favors by bringing him illegal marijuana. Even if he doesn't get hooked, they'll probably throw his butt in jail."

"He's dying, Tricia. Lots of pain. They can't do anything for him... or won't. I'm just trying to provide him a little relief." A lump in his throat. "Lieutenant Tyler was a fighter pilot during World War Two. Flew P-47 combat missions but that doesn't get him any pain pills which actually work. I just want to help."

Even though I didn't know Ralph, my eyes leaked, because I remembered visiting my great-grandfather—also a greatest generation vet—as he was dying in the hospital. "Oh."

Mike took a deep breath, as if for control. "One of the many things that impressed me about Lieutenant Tyler was while he was training in Kansas his P-47's engine caught fire. Obviously, the instinct is to bail out as soon as you reach the right altitude. But he nearly rode that plane into the ground because he was trying to avoid crashing into some houses."

"What happened?" My own throat tightened at the

story.

"He was able to crash it in a field. Got badly burned and barely had enough air to open his chute."

I'd placed my fingertips on Mike's left thigh before my brain realized what I was doing. He just glanced out of the corner of his eye but made no comment. My face felt warm as I looked the other way and removed my hand, trying to pretend it was never there. "I comprehend what you're doing and why, but that doesn't make it any less dangerous. And it's still illegal in this state."

"So you understand why I wasn't eager to confab with those officers."

"Yeah. But *you've* also got to understand something. I'm not going to jail for the sake of your noble lieutenant friend. If we do get stopped, you'd better toss that marijuana out the window... or swallow it."

"Way too much to swallow."

Which made *me* swallow hard. "Mike, exactly how much grass do you have in that duffle?"

He held his hands in the approximate dimensions of a medium cereal bowl. I dared not ask how high that virtual bowl was piled with actual illegal pot.

I'm afraid I produced more unconnected syllables. Some of those sputters noted that not only had my timetable and predictability been blown out of the water, but now I was complicit in a drug-running scheme. "What next? Arson?"

"Settle down, Tricia. We're on a road nobody uses... so you said. It's late Sunday night and nobody's out. From here, it should be clear sailing to Verdeville. Right?"

Except for that odor, the one I'd started worrying about. Not a good time for car troubles, not with the work-related disaster awaiting me tomorrow morning. But all I could do was reluctantly nod. To paraphrase Auntie, it would be uncautious of me to utter the words "clear sailing."

"Okay, so we've settled everything?"

Whatever.

As he began sniffing, presumably the same smell I'd noticed, he checked his mirror. So did I. A large tractor-trailer pulled over to the shoulder about half a mile behind us. "It's suddenly getting kind of crowded out here. Let's get moving to Verdeville."

I looked behind us—lots of activity back there. At least one other vehicle, maybe two, pulled in behind the big rig and several men scrambled out. "Okay, to home base." When I turned the ignition key, it started but sounded funny. And the odor was more distinct—something rusty and burning. My eye caught one of the dashboard warning lights.

"What's the problem? Let's go."

"Not sure. Odd smell." I pointed to the indicator light. "What does that one mean?"

Mike took a few deep breaths and wrinkled his nose. "Hmm." Then he leaned way over, his face practically in my lap, and studied the dash display. "That's the temperature symbol. You're overheating."

I sure was, but only because his left cheek rested upon my thigh. "What do you mean?" When he turned to face me, his nose brushed against my right breast. I knew immediately it was untoward to feel turned on by a third cousin-in-law twice removed, but I couldn't help it. Also couldn't recall the last time a man's face had been near either region of my body. It was a specific high-voltage electric current which hadn't been plugged in for a long time.

"Pop the hood. I need to see what's what." He banged his head on the steering wheel as he lurched up off my lap.

Then he quickly peered out the rear window toward the vehicles and men. "On second thought, just drive on. Maybe we'll find a place down the road."

"I think we're leaving the last place in town, Mike." Stronger smell, worse sound.

"Well, get moving, quick." Another whip around to check behind us. "I've seen all of Hermitage I want to see."

I engaged drive and accelerated. The Toyota made a valiant effort, but hardly half a mile further it conked out... with steam rising from under the hood. "Mike!" When I pointed, I realized my hand was shaking.

"Could be the water pump, maybe fan belt, or even a thermostat."

"Can you fix it?"

"Not here in the dark, not without tools and parts. And not when we're crowded by people behind us."

"Let's go ask them for help."

"Don't think so, Tricia." He jumped from the car, retrieved his duffle from the back seat, and motioned for me to pop the trunk.

I did, then also exited and watched as Mike shoved the duffle as far up in the trunk as he could reach. Then he pulled it back enough to open the top and remove a large revolver in a pancake style holster.

I'd been around guns since I was a teen and am never bothered by them when they're in my own hands. But when somebody whips one out of nowhere, I tend to tense up like I'd just heard a rattlesnake. "What's that for?"

"I've got a bad feeling about our friends back there."

5

10:42 p.m.

Stunned by the sight of that massive firearm—in the hands of someone I scarcely knew—I could barely focus on Mike's barrage of questions.

"How far are we now from where we dropped off Shondell?" he asked, with one eye on the men and vehicles behind us.

"Uh, her grannie's place is maybe a dozen miles back." I tend to monitor the odometer for some obsessive reason.

"So you've got a pretty good idea of where we are?"

Not really… difficult to get my bearings at night. "A few more miles to the county line, I think, then maybe ten more to Marrowbone."

"Marrowbone?"

"Yeah. Just a little community, actually. It's maybe five or six miles along 70, past the road to Mount Juliet."

"Know much about it?" He checked again behind us.

"Hold on. First, tell me the reason you've got a gun and

why you act like you're ready to use it."

"Later. Marrowbone." His clipped words drove the conversation where he wanted it to go.

Wasn't at all comfortable with the idea of waiting for his explanation, but I sensed Mike wouldn't be swayed. Rather than argue, I relented. "I went to school with a guy who lives outside Marrowbone. He works over here... not far from where we would've caught the ramp to I-40."

"You trust him?" Laidback, easygoing Mike had tensed considerably in the past minutes.

The pounding of my heart seemed too fast and too loud. "Not if he was in bed with me, but in every other way." My face flushed as I spoke. *Don't know why I said that.*

"Well, let's head to Marrowbone and look up your buddy." Another quick glance rearward. "And fast."

"On foot? Over ten miles? At night?"

"Grab your purse, lock the car, and let's go. Now." He slid the holster flap inside his waistband and the gun hung there like it was a frequent companion. The only way that would have comforted me was if he were an officer, which clearly he wasn't, since we'd backtracked just to avoid the police.

I did as instructed, however, and Mike hustled me along the north side shoulder, heading east beside Highway 24. I wondered if I could make it on foot even to the county line, where it would be designated Highway 70. Couldn't believe I'd left my sweater in the car.

We'd gone barely a mile—which took us probably ten minutes—when distant headlights shone on our backsides.

"Act like we live here." He grabbed my hand. "We're just a couple out for a moonlight walk and we're going home. Keep walking... 'til I say run."

I squinted at him. He seemed serious. "Run? But we don't know who it is."

"It's those guys behind us, where your car died."

"How do you know?" My head pounded with tension to match my overactive pulse. So much strange behavior from a guy I'd barely met. Part of me wanted to jerk my hand away and turn back to the car. But the headlights lit us up from behind, stark and bright, and my fright wouldn't let me release his hand. Whatever was going on, I didn't want to leave his side.

Mike shrugged and his fingers gripped mine. "Call it a gut feeling... 99 per cent certain."

"Maybe they can help us."

He set his jaw. "No way."

"How can you be so positive?" Whenever people were that certain, it made me extra worried they knew something I didn't.

"Because they're stealing whatever cargo's on that big truck." His voice rumbled low, like the muffled diesel creeping toward us.

"Hijackers?" My belly cramped and made me nearly forget my head pain. No, he had to be wrong. "I don't believe it."

"You will if they catch up to us." He grabbed my elbow roughly as the headlights got closer and brighter. "In the ditch and let's lose them in these trees. Now. Run!"

No words to describe my dismay, confusion, and terror. Once, when I'd been a kid, a carnival ride had terrified me, swooping so close to the ground and whirling like it was going to pitch me into space. My dad had successfully begged the attendant to stop the ride and let his screeching daughter off. No way to extricate myself from this ride, however.

Something shivery whispered in my ear that we were strapped in for the duration.

Weeds, briars, and limbs tore at me, ripping at my arms and jeans. My strappy flats slid through the forest mulch and I stumbled again and again. Only Mike's grip on my hand kept me upright. I struggled to keep up with him, but he seemed like a Deerstalker character who'd spent his whole life in the wilderness. He ran like a sprinter through the brush and somehow never made a sound nor put a foot wrong. Panting, I begged him to slow down.

"Quiet!" he hissed, then halted abruptly and squatted right where he'd stopped. "Listen."

"To what?" I whispered, trying to control my rough panting.

"Are they following us?"

My ears don't work as well when my guts are churning with fear and my eyes are squeezing back tears. But I tried. "Don't hear anything. No headlights either."

"Same for me."

Gasping for breath, I reached for his forearm. "So that's good news. Right?"

"Maybe." He raised his face like a wild animal smelling for his enemies. "Or could be bad."

My heart rate tripled, again. "How could it be bad news if they're *not* following us?"

"The bad news is we don't know where they are. Wish they'd turn those headlights back on."

"Wait. Wait. Mike, wait." I clutched again at his arm, like he was the only one who could pull me out of quicksand. "You've got to give me something to go on here." I was pleading. "Why are we running and why would those guys care either way?"

Through the low canopy of confining woods, the mocking moonlight revealed only a shadowy glimpse of his expression—disbelief. He couldn't comprehend that I didn't comprehend. "They care because we're witnesses."

"To what? I didn't see a thing," I whispered hoarsely. "And I don't think you saw anything, either." My fingernails dug into his arm. I had to hang on somehow. "You're basically guessing what they were up to."

After another deep breath in and out, he leaned closer, his face inches away from mine. "There's no reason for a big truck to be where that one was, at this time of night. No sense in the other vehicles pulling in and all those guys jumping out and messing with the cargo rig. Since there's no innocent explanation, their purpose has to be otherwise." His voice couldn't have been heard a foot away.

"But that's still mostly conjecture." I was begging for it to be untrue, and suddenly I realized that he'd convinced me and I hadn't even noticed.

"Hush." Mike crouched lower and yanked me further down beside him, his hand gripping my shoulder. "Did you hear that?"

Something. Not sure what. "Maybe the wind."

"Which direction?"

Couldn't tell. Barely knew up from down. "I no longer know which way Marrowbone is."

"I don't think they're behind us, but I know they're close."

I wanted to shake him 'til he said something I could tolerate. "How?"

"I can feel them."

Good grief. Was my twice-removed third cousin-in-law also a psychic? "Where?"

"Not sure. Let's go." He lugged up my limp body and began running again... hopefully east. I had no more idea of our actual direction than I'd had as a kid on that horrifying carnival ride. Could've been endless circles.

We ran, Mike tugging me behind him. Air burned through my heaving lungs and my side cramped, but my legs kept pumping. He slid past brush and brambles, hardly making them sway; I staggered through, thorns snagging in my arms and jeans.

A few steps later, my feet slid on dead leaves. Legs gave out and I started to fall. Mike released my hand. Before I had time to panic, before my knees even hit the ground, his strong arm wrapped around my waist. Without seeming to slow down, he heaved me upright and kept moving. Despite my exhaustion and terror, in his grasp I somehow managed to keep going.

After what seemed like painful forever, Mike halted again and dropped to the ground. Even with his arm around me, I basically fell on top of him, gasping for air. My legs were screaming and my arms and face stung with cuts. When I rolled off him, my butt landed in a low wet spot. *Yuck.* "What now?"

"I heard a vehicle. Sounded like over there." He nodded over his right shoulder.

"Is the highway still that direction?" I was clueless.

"Yeah. We're running basically parallel, but I'm also trying to put a little more distance between us and the road."

Wondered how he could even see the highway, but I was too exhausted to ask... and it wouldn't have made any difference. Didn't even look, somehow sensing if I kept my eyes closed, I might control my terror.

Mike got my attention and pointed ahead, presumably

east. "I think there's a clearing or something up there. Hoping it's for a power line." Again he inhaled deeply. "Any small roads coming off that highway, going north?"

"Don't know." Chest still heaving and lungs burning, I clutched his sweaty hand. "Look, I've never been in these woods before. I've only seen them from the highway. And I've probably only driven this stretch of highway about three or four times in my whole life. Could be lots of side roads... maybe none." Hot tears burned down my cheeks as I tried to quell the tremor in my voice. "I just don't know, Mike. I'm mostly acquainted with this general area because I've been to Marrowbone a few times and because Uncle Cleve has a big Greene County map on his wall."

"Have we crossed the county line yet?"

"Might have. Maybe not." I groaned. "How could we tell?"

He seemed to dismiss my question as he cocked his ears again. "I need to go see what kind of clearing that is and if we can cross it safely." He stood. "You stay here."

Panic. "Not on your life, Mike." I grabbed his leg as I struggled to stand on my own. "I've seen too many movies where the woman stays put. It never comes out good."

Exasperation. "Well, if you're coming with me, you have to be quiet."

I'm always quiet... except when I'm running for my life in the dense woods at night with an armed man I've never set eyes on until a couple of hours ago. To him, I said nothing.

Mike slowed as we neared the clear stretch, which was evidently a minor farm road jutting north from the highway. He dropped again to a crouch and pulled me with him.

I staggered, then collapsed beside him. My arms were covered with goose bumps and my body shook, but I was grateful we weren't still running.

"Road," he hissed.

I didn't share his obvious dismay, figuring it would be a lot easier walking along a thoroughfare than stumbling through dark thorny woods. "What's the problem?" Now my teeth chattered, but not from cold.

No answer while he sniffed the air like a tracking wolf. "I'd sure like to know where those guys are," he whispered hoarsely.

"Probably way back down the highway," I said, trying to point, but my hand shook too badly. "Probably right outside Hermitage where we left them."

"Don't think so. They were right behind us before we broke into the woods." He took the deepest breath I'd ever seen, though I might've missed most of the others in our frantic run through unknown darkness. "They weren't planning on any witnesses."

Why couldn't it be simple and sane?

Mike grabbed me again. "Let's go. Slow and quiet."

Slow was easy enough because I was so exhausted, but quiet was impossible. My heavy breathing alone would alert anyone nearby.

We had scarcely reached the edge of the woods when bright lights blinded us, somebody grabbed me, Mike was knocked to the ground, and two guys wrestled away his gun.

6

11:07 p.m.

My terror went beyond panic, confusion, and the uncertainty of what might happen next. This fear was immediate, intense, and it *knew*. No doubts. Far worse than the fear of *maybe something bad could happen*. We were right in the middle of *it's happening now*. That knowledge reached deep inside me, wrapped its icy fists around my brain and heart, and squeezed until something popped, leaving me voiceless and nearly paralyzed. As rough hands clutched at my body, I could do nothing.

The next several minutes were a blur of coarse voices, harsh handling, and—most of the time—lights in my eyes so I could only see shapeless forms. We were both alive, so far, and tossed into the back of a diesel pickup, where three of the punks kept us pinned down with guns as the truck turned back onto Highway 24. The man on me, with one boot pressed atop my ribs, deliberately rubbed against my breasts. The pickup jolted, rumbled for a distance, then slowed and stopped. With our heads below the truck bed's sides, we couldn't know where we were.

The single *good* factor I could discern—besides both of us still breathing—was considerable confusion among the felons who'd captured us. Mike and I were thumped each time we attempted to communicate, so I don't know if I came up with this myself or if it was through some sort of ESP from him. But I suddenly became convinced their confusion arose from what to do with us. In other words, they had not yet decided to kill us. Not definitely.

Small comfort, but I had to latch onto whatever I could. Otherwise I'd be worse off than just paralyzed with terror.

Finally we were back on the outskirts of Hermitage. I spotted my car about a mile in the distance as we were both yanked from the pickup and dragged to the ditch on the south side of the highway, behind the tractor-trailer. None too gently, and the one tugging on me managed to grope my chest and butt repeatedly. Survival instinct began to emerge through tiny cracks in my paralyzing terror, and I was startled to realize part of that instinct was anger. But if we were to both survive, our fear and rage must be controlled by strategy.

"Hold on, guys," said Mike, sounding surprisingly calm. "We've got no interest in your operation here. We don't know your names and haven't seen your faces hardly."

"Shut him up," said the leader, stocky, sturdy, short, and snarly. Couldn't see his face and didn't want to.

When a minion elbowed Mike's head, the impact echoed inside me. I wanted to belt him back.

"Listen to me," Mike continued after recovering from the blow. "Whatever's going on with this truck cargo is just theft. But if you involve us, that's kidnapping... which is federal."

"So is taking this cargo, Jack." When Mr. Big stomped closer and glared, I finally saw his face—like a prizefighter who'd battled a chainsaw. I turned away in disgust.

Mike warily monitored both the leader and guard, likely expecting another whack. "Look. I'm not arguing legal points. I'm just saying you don't need kidnapping added to whatever else is going on." He drew a ragged breath. "We don't know anything and don't want to."

Behind the leader continued a flurry of activity—the remaining four men carefully unloading massive crated motorcycles and loading them on small trailers, four per trailer. They should've brought a forklift or hijacked a rig with a lift gate.

Mr. Big watched our eyes. "You've got a pretty good idea what's up." He pointed to Mike's holster. "Hand that over. I like my new revolver and need some good leather for it."

Mike struggled to remove the empty pancake holster's retainer from inside his britches—evidently it was difficult from a seated position. Then he held it up.

"Toss it over... real gentle."

He did.

One of the minions hustled over and whispered in Mr. Big's ear. Whatever he said angered the leader. "No! Doesn't matter." He shoved the man's shoulder. "Git back to work." Then Mr. Big reached down to pick up the holster. "Sweet."

"Where's my revolver?" asked Mike quietly.

Mr. Big held it up with an admiring appraisal, then holstered it. "You won't need it any more, Jack."

Without addressing us further, the boss told the man guarding us to be vigilant—not his wording, though—or he'd be in more trouble than we were. The sentry understood. Then Mr. Big spat loudly onto the pavement and stalked back toward the manual unloading operation.

We were about fifty feet behind the big truck, where frantic activity was punctuated by harsh cursing and violent cuffs from the leader. One of the crates fell, slamming to the road's shoulder and cracking several boards like they'd been smacked with a sledgehammer. As Mr. Big freaked and cursed, two of the workers shoved that motorcycle to one side.

Though I was new to hijacking, it was already obvious they had not brought enough small trucks and trailers. There appeared to be roughly three dozen motorcycles in that rig and each of the two trailers held only four. I wondered why they were even transferring the cargo, but figured it must have related to how traceable they'd be in that larger vehicle. Anyway, it would take at least four loads apiece for those smaller trucks to carry the entire cargo to wherever they were going. I could only hope that destination was far away, because I'd already decided our lifespan might only be as long as it took them to complete their theft.

After all the kicks and other thumps, I'd made no further effort to speak with Mike but could sense he was calculating escape and evasion plans. I had no ideas whatsoever, but knew one thing for certain—I'd go with him, anywhere, anyhow. So I had to be ready.

"Where's the driver?" Mike asked Sentry.

"Shut up." It was a whispered growl.

"Just tell me if he's dead or wounded, dude."

"Knocked out cold. That's all. Boss was trying to keep it clean." Sentry spat. "'Til you two showed up."

"I'm telling you we're easy. Didn't see anything, don't

know anything." He wriggled his hips on the ground to get closer to the guard. "If the driver's still alive and you let us go, you guys are still in pretty good shape. Get your cash for the cargo, and you're free and clear."

"Maybe." Sentry grunted. "But the boss says you're staying."

"Just take us to the driver. My wife's a nurse."

Wife? Nurse? A strange chill shivered up my spine. *What crazy scheme is he working up?*

"Keep quiet." He kicked Mike, though with less impact than previously. "The boss is busy over there and that's better for all of us."

"Okay, but just tell us where the driver is."

"Why do ya care?"

I was wondering the same thing. All I could figure was Mike wanted to shift the guard's attention off us.

"I told you, dude, my wife's a nurse. It's to your benefit to keep that driver alive."

Sentry waggled the pistol barrel slightly. "Knock it off."

When Mr. Big stalked over and pulled Sentry aside, I could only hear bits and pieces. It appeared we were temporarily being left behind with the single guard while the others went with the first two trailer loads and then returned with either more trailers or larger ones. Evidently they wanted to get the remaining cargo—over two dozen more bikes, by my guesswork—in one final load.

I watched Mike melt to the ground, as though to say *We're no problem... one guard is plenty.* I didn't need to pretend any melting, since I was already a pitiful heap... and the seat of my jeans was wet from that puddle.

"We'll be back in fifteen or less," whispered Mr. Big. "If they give you any trouble, bust his head open."

Sentry nodded.

"I'm taking the rig's keys, just in case anybody decides to git creative." Then Big's volume increased. "And keep your hands off the girl," he said with a vile gleam. "She's mine."

I shuddered. Couldn't help it. The thought of his meaty paws all over me and his evil, scarred face in mine just freaked me. But Mike didn't move a muscle.

The leader let out a hollow laugh and turned back toward the rear of the tractor-trailer. Shortly Mr. Big and his four other minions piled into the two small trucks and drove back toward Hermitage proper. I assumed they had a staging area somewhere south of town, where it would be fairly quick and easy to jump on I-40 and head east or west to wherever they'd meet their buyers.

I ached all over, from exhaustion and our struggle in the woods plus the battering from these criminals. And I couldn't help thinking none of this would've happened if Mike hadn't rescued Shondell back at the gas station. *In other words, because she's better off, I'm worse off.* Ironic how we'd traded places: an hour ago, Shondell was being abused and we'd helped her. Now we were the victims, and no rescuers within miles. I trembled—couldn't help it. *Mike better have an escape plan.* He *had* to... because I had nothing.

After Big and the others drove away, I felt about ten times better—temporarily. Still scared to death, but realizing we had nearly fifteen minutes for Mike to pull an escape rabbit out of his hat. Mike's eyes bored into mine and I knew he was thinking the same thing. Whatever happened would be quick and there'd be no time for me to ask questions—I had to be ready to jump. So I didn't take my eyes off him, not even to blink.

"Now that the boss isn't breathing down your neck, let's go check on that driver."

"Shut up." Sentry waggled his pistol.

"I think I heard him moaning, dude." Mike moved ever so slightly, as though he might be situating his muscles for something sudden. "If he's moaning, that means he's awake now. Unless you've got him hog-tied, he could be on his way over here to help us."

A vigorous kick into Mike's hip. "Keep quiet."

The blow obviously hurt but didn't shake Mike from his strategy. "Okay, okay. Just trying to help you out. I think you're a lot smarter than those other guys and I'd hate to see you take the fall for the rest of them."

"What do ya mean?"

"Well, if it was me they left behind with two hostages and a dead guy, I'd be a little worried that I was holding the bag, if you get my drift."

"They're coming back with more trailers." He peered anxiously in the direction they'd gone. "Besides, I ain't holding nothing… and the driver ain't dead. Not yet."

"A smart operator would check it out. Don't want your boss coming back and finding that driver standing over your dead body with a tire iron in his bloody hands. Think of the trouble you'd be in."

"I told you to shut… up." And the guard whipped back his leg to unleash a vicious kick.

In the same nano-speed I'd witnessed at the gas station, Mike altered position, used his own leg to catch the guard's… and the combined energy of both movements flipped the felon over. He landed on his back with an agonizing thud and Mike pounced on top. Three or four brutal blows and Sentry was out, his pistol resting loosely in a limp hand.

"We're going." He grabbed the pistol and yanked me up. "Now."

I was too stunned—my legs wouldn't move. Other than Shondell's cuffing, I'd never seen any real-life violence—the stuff in movies was distant and detached. But this was up close and personal. And bloody. "Going where?" *Stupid question, Tricia—anywhere away from this deathtrap!*

"Get the keys from the rig's cab."

"What keys? He took the one for the truck."

"To the bikes. And don't leave any fingerprints in that truck." When he returned his brutally efficient attention to the guard, I didn't stick around to watch.

Already knew I'd do whatever he'd say, so I didn't waste any breath with questions or argument. To keep my prints to myself, I covered one hand with the tail of my blouse. By the time I'd rummaged through the cab, located a large brown envelope with some three dozen sets of keys, and returned to the back of the rig, Mike had wrestled the set-aside Harley-Davidson motorcycle out of its wooden crate.

"Find the key that ends in 1207," he said. "I'm gonna check on the driver."

It was the ninth or tenth set I examined with fabric-covered fingertips.

Mike returned, shaking his head.

"Here… 1207. How's the driver?"

"Already dead."

My tears were mostly prompted by the shock, I guess, since I'd never even seen the driver. I hadn't been around many murder victims, either. "I thought…"

"Don't think the guard even knew." Mike hopped on the bike, turned the key, and the engine roared. "Their leader evidently believes in compartmentalization." He handed me the pistol after engaging the safety. "Put this in your bag. Let's go."

I did. Then I jumped on back, tucked my purse in front of my belly, and wrapped my arms around my twice-removed third cousin-in-law. "Okay."

The shock of takeoff sent ice down to my guts. I'd been on scooters and trail bikes before, but this Harley-Davidson launched us like a fiery rocket.

"What kind of bike is this?" I yelled.

"Electra Glide Ultra Classic with 1690 cc's of power," he shouted back.

I felt every surge of that incredible engine as it blew us down the highway. When Mike headed east, I ducked my face between his meaty shoulder blades and held on tightly. Can't say I felt safe and certainly not comfortable, but I had a sense of relieved adrenaline that we'd somehow dodged a bullet—quite literally.

"We're gonna need gas real quick," he yelled over his shoulder. "These are tested at the factory but they're shipped with hardly more than fumes. What's open on Sunday nights?"

"About halfway to Marrowbone is the highway coming north from Mount Juliet," I shouted into the frigid rushing air. "If we don't find anything before then, there's probably a station at that intersection."

"Okay. I want to get as far as we can as quick as possible. Hang on."

I did. For my life.

7

11:32 p.m.

Thankfully, there was a convenience store along Highway 70, about halfway between the Greene County line and the intersection with the artery to Mount Juliet. Only one gas pump but it was open.

Our bedraggled condition clearly alarmed the clerk, but she said nothing—she'd probably seen even worse. I hoped they didn't have any surveillance cameras, but not for the usual reasons. When I got to the cracked mirror inside the restroom, I nearly bawled. My face was streaked with tears and blood... hair was a tangled mess. My clothes were torn and the briars had ripped into my legs, arms, and neck. The cuts themselves burned individually, but all my joints felt like I'd been tossed into an industrial dryer and tumbled on rough cycle for an hour.

Mike wasn't much different, but he's a guy and they look a whole lot better in blood and grime. So unfair.

Since he'd given all his folding money to Shondell's

grannie, I had to pay for the gasoline. He told me not to use a credit card, so we just put in $13.74 worth—about two-thirds of the six-gallon tank. I was careful not to reveal the confiscated pistol as I fished for my cash.

Also realized I was starving. When Mike noticed me drooling, he dug from his pocket enough change—when supplemented by three pennies we claimed from the little "give one / take one" saucer in front of the register—for one candy bar. He unwrapped it, broke it in two, and held out both pieces. I took the nearest one and scarfed it down in three bites. Don't think I did much chewing either.

The clerk continued to give us the fisheye, but did not seem actually frightened. Extremely puzzled, however. "So, you guys been in a wreck?"

"Yeah," replied Mike. "Hit a slick spot back there and took a tumble. But we're okay."

"If you say so." She returned her primary attention to the low-volume TV show she'd been monitoring, but kept easing one eye back toward us for the additional minute we remained inside.

Stepping through the doors and out of the clerk's earshot, I asked Mike, "Tell me again what kind of trouble we're in after stealing a motorcycle from those bikers?"

"First of all, they aren't bikers. If they'd been bikers, they probably would've helped me get your car running. No, those guys were thieves. And I didn't steal anything from them, because it wasn't theirs. They were ripping off that truck."

It felt like we were arguing in circles, but I was genuinely confused. "Then you stole it from the truck."

"Nope. It was already stolen. On the ground in a busted crate behind the truck. We rescued it from the thieves. And when we get your car back, maybe we can return Number 1207 to one of the dealerships it was heading to in Nashville."

What else could happen? "How do you know where it was going?"

"Tricia, you're sweating the small stuff. Right now we've got to get to a safe spot and figure out how to get your car back."

Despite his words, my brain kept processing the variables: *Would I ever see my car again? Was my car more valuable than my job... or my life? Should we call the police? Would they notice the marijuana in the duffle bag?*

Mike looked back toward the west. "Don't want to lose any more time here. You okay to keep going?"

"What do you mean?"

"You look cold."

"I am, but that's not why I'm shivering."

He started to say something, but never spat it out. "All right, jump on and let's roll."

Mike cranked the engine and revved it. Under other circumstances, it could have been a mellow rumbling refrain, but at present, it sounded more like the pounding hoofbeats of 76 getaway horses. "Okay."

He left the parking lot slowly, which shouldn't arouse the clerk's attention, but when he'd gone a quarter mile east on Highway 70, he opened the throttle wide. "Can you get us to your friend's house in the dark?" he yelled over his shoulder.

Hanging on to my twice-removed third cousin-in-law with all the strength my rubbery arms still possessed, I shouted into his broad shoulders, "Ought to be about ten miles from this next intersection. Maybe less."

"Is it marked?"

"One blinking light... but sometimes they have it turned off." Wasn't sure how much of my explanation he heard, but I figured I could get his attention when I spotted the turn.

At 85 miles per hour, the night air was positively freezing even though it was only late September, and I wished I'd been able to grab my sweater from the stranded Toyota. But that desperate flight, along with the gas station rescue of Shondell and my initial encounter with Mike at the bus station, was all a lifetime ago. As I snuggled into Mike's muscular body, for both safety and partial warmth, I had the distinct panicky feeling my stressful night was not nearly over.

Don't think it's possible to doze off on the back of a Harley at that speed, but maybe I fainted for five minutes, because the next thing I knew, we were approaching the un-blinking blinking light which signaled the village of Marrowbone. Well, not officially a village because it didn't have even that many people, but everybody called it such.

I squeezed hard on Mike's midsection to get his attention. "Slow down," I yelled. "Next right."

"South?"

"Yeah." In the middle of my screamed reply, the Harley's powerful engine dropped rpms to a fraction of what we'd been doing and suddenly I could converse in reasonable volume. "After you cross the tracks, hang a left."

Across the railroad bed, but before turning east, Mike pulled over and throttled down to an idle again. "How much further?"

"Maybe a mile down this road, then we turn south again for about half a mile."

"Crowded neighborhood?" He was acting as he did

when we'd approached the bus station parking lot—needing to know what was ahead before he stuck his neck into it.

"No. His is the only house out that way... or used to be."

Just as I was about to inquire again what he planned to do with this hot Harley, Mike asked me, "Know anybody who needs a bike and doesn't care where it came from?"

"Only one person comes to mind—the guy we're going to see, Eric Prima. He can fix anything and rides everything."

"So how do you know this guy?" He sounded more jealous than curious.

A vaguely satisfied fuzzy feeling burst through the cold, warming me from within. "Like I told you, we went to school together... in Verdeville."

"So he's not an ex-boyfriend?"

"Eric's an ex about a hundred times over." I laughed. When Mike scooted forward on his seat, turned, and faced me with a frown, I explained. "He's had a long string of girls and I never wanted to be just one more catch on his stringer. But he's a good guy and a great friend."

"And you're positive we can trust him?"

"As much as I trust you, Mike—with my life."

Seated properly again, he smiled over his broad shoulder... a confident smile without brashness. "Okay, Eric it is. Hang on." Mike followed my previous directions and about three minutes later we were near enough to see Eric's front porch light. Other than using his bathroom, I hoped I could borrow a warm blanket.

Eric was rocking on his porch, petting his homely dog with one hand and holding what was probably a gun magazine with the other. He was only pretending to read, however, because he was clearly monitoring our approaching chopper. His porch light cast shadows in several directions, but I could make out a long firearm leaning against the door frame, within easy reach.

Mike stopped the bike about sixty feet away. His jaw and shoulders tensed, like he anticipated making a quick turn-around.

I jumped off. "Give me a minute to say hello. You'd better wait here."

Without taking his eyes off the porch, Mike nodded.

Back in high school, I'd had a furious schoolgirl freshman crush on Eric Prima. I'd lurked and lusted. Eric had also been interested in me, but when he'd learned I was at least three years younger, he'd kept our relationship at the friend gate and would not allow himself to jump over. It had hurt at age fifteen—nearly everything does—but since getting over it, I'd realized how noble he'd been not to take things further. But I'd always wondered what it might've been like...

"Eric? It's me, Tricia Pilgrim." I approached, holding my empty hands out to each side. "Went to school together... Verdeville High."

One hand kept scratching the dog's head, but Eric's other hand released the magazine and rose in a lazy wave. "Tricia! How you doin'?" From the sound of his voice, he probably had a couple of beers in him.

Seeing his big smile, I approached the porch, and Eric slowly stood. The front door opened and his girlfriend Velma peered around the corner. She was in her bra and panties, so I wondered if we'd interrupted something important.

"I've been better," I answered, but surely he could see that as I reached his steps.

He gazed over me slowly. His eyes also reflected alcohol consumption, but they still sharply took in my battered appearance. The sudden creases in his brow indicated concern, but also an air of resignation. "It is what it is," Eric intoned solemnly. He'd been saying that since high school.

8

11:51 p.m.

"Who's that?" Eric pointed toward the waiting, rumbling chopper.

"My, uh, third cousin-in-law twice removed," I explained, "on Aunt Mary's side."

Eric waved him in and addressed me again even though his eyes remained on Mike. "Are you hurt bad, Tricia?"

"Mostly scrapes, cuts, and bruises." My eyes welled up with the list. "But I'm pretty durn cold."

"Velma, you got a blanket in there?" he called over his shoulder without taking his gaze off Mike, now approaching the porch. "You two in trouble somehow?"

Velma, still attired in her intimates, reappeared and stared as she handed over a small, thin blanket throw. I wrapped it around myself but couldn't help staring at *her.*

And Mike's eyes were similarly glued because Velma, though lacking fundamental modesty, had everything else in spades. Nicely formed and evidently eager to please Eric.

I'd heard Eric previously say they were "80 per cent" married... whatever that meant.

When Mike mounted the porch steps, I introduced him. "This is Cousin Michael."

"Mike," he corrected me. They shook hands, with evidently more grip than either needed and for slightly longer than was necessary. I figured it was like two roosters trying to decide who was alpha.

Velma—a former exotic dancer, I'd been told—lazily scratched her hip as she watched.

"Velma, go make some coffee, will ya, hon? These folks've been on the road a bit." Eric swatted her butt. "And put some clothes on."

"Could I use your restroom?" I asked.

"Sure, you go ahead. It's still in the same perzack place." He winked at Mike when he said it. "Me and your cousin'll get acquainted."

That sounded slightly ominous to me, but the restroom call was more urgent, so I hurriedly tended it. By the time I returned to the porch, Mike and Eric were sitting and chatting like old buddies.

"...slap my keester on a hot grill!" chuckled Eric. "That's a doozy."

I could only guess Mike had been describing our breakdown and capture and escape. But I did *not* consider any of that in the category of a *doozy*. "By the way, Eric, how come you're out on your porch this close to midnight?" I asked as I plopped into a chair and wrapped the throw around me again. "I'd figure you two would be in bed by now." When I realized what I'd said, I blushed.

Eric pretended not to notice. "Well, Daisy-Dawg there," he pointed to the Catahoula Cur, "came up to me about half an hour ago and said somebody was coming to visit."

"You're kidding... right?" Mike was already grinning.

"Well, she doesn't talk out loud, but that's what she means when she comes over like that. No barking, no whining... just the thing she does with the pitch of her ears."

"Eric, how would your dog know visitors were on their way?" I asked. "A half hour ago, we were in the woods near Hermitage."

"She knows. Ain't that right, Daisy-Dawg?"

The dog kept her own counsel.

"How?" asked Mike.

Eric frowned as though we'd missed a key lesson in school science. "Daisy-Dawg's a psychic."

I'd never heard of a psychic dog and it seemed Mike hadn't either.

Eric must have sensed our skepticism. "Well, it's pretty rare. I bet you won't find one in a hundred thousand. But oddly enough, the Catahoula Cur has it more than any other breed."

Okay, I'll bite. "Why?"

"Something to do with their spots and their eyes. I don't know perzackly." Then he smiled. With Eric, you never knew when he was joshing. After checking through the screen door on the status of the coffee, he asked, "What brings y'all way out here to Marrowbone?"

Maybe they hadn't already discussed it after all, which made me wonder all the more which "doozy" Eric had been chuckling about. Since Mike looked at me, I figured I was the official reporter, so I explained hurriedly. Skimmed through the gas station incident and didn't even mention our run through the woods or the stop at the convenience store. Focused mainly on our encounter with the gang of

Harley thieves and the fact that my car was stranded back at the scene. "On top of everything else, I've got to be at work at 9 a.m. for a big surprise audit."

Ignoring my work-related misery, Eric opened his eyes wide and smiled. "Y'all need help bustin' up any crooks? I can get two guys here in ten minutes. Four, if you're willing to wait a bit longer."

I reached over and patted his wrist. "I don't think we need your whole gang…"

"Let the man talk, Tricia," interrupted Mike. "Never turn down good help. A squad's better than a patrol."

Eric nodded. "Military?"

"Army," replied Mike with no elaboration.

I hadn't heard about that from Aunt Mary. "All we need is somebody to drive us over to my car in Hermitage and fix the *whatever* so we can get on our way."

Seemingly ignoring me, Eric had watched Mike's face as I'd spoken. "I can borrow my buddy's wrecker and if it's simple, we can fix it here."

"Probably just the thermostat, judging from the smell," interjected Mike, "but maybe a hose or water pump. It was dark and we were in a hurry to get away."

Velma came out with the coffee and three cups. The only item she'd added to her outfit was an apron. She seemed peeved at having visitors. "Y'all need anything else?"

"Don't think so, hon." He tried to swat her derrière as she walked past him, but she dodged. The view when she turned was impressive. "I might be going out later, Velma."

"I'll be sound asleep when you get back." She let the screen door slam behind her as she returned to the house.

Eric grinned as he whispered, "She'll get over it." Then his face straightened. "Now back up to this gang of chopper thieves."

Mike nodded enthusiastically.

I began shaking my head. "Wait a minute. We're not tangling with *them* again. We barely got out alive." I looked from face to face. "I just need my car back."

"And I need my stuff," added Mike. "But those punks stole a truckload of Harleys and killed the driver. They need some manners."

"That's perzackly what I was thinking, cousin."

"Guys, listen to reason." With the hand not holding coffee, I clutched at Mike's arm. "This is a matter for the police."

"Not until I get my duffle out of your car, Tricia."

"Oh… yeah. Forgot."

Eric's eyes lit up. "So what's in that duffle, cousin?"

"Let's call it medicinal and it's not for me." Then Mike explained its destination and purpose.

"Well, we can't let a World War Two vet suffer when you've got some relief parked right there in Hermitage," concluded Eric. "What's your plan?"

"Plan?" I shrieked. "Absolutely no plan. No more tangling with hijackers, period." I tried to take a deep breath but my lungs wouldn't work. "We drive in, snatch my car, and drive out."

Mike faced me and spoke slowly, calmly. "We're witnesses to the theft and we know they killed the driver. If we don't go after them, they'll still be coming after us."

Eric nodded. "He's right, Tricia. It is what it is. And there's been some other trucks jumped around here. Can't swear it's these same guys, but one of our shipments for my parts store was on a truck that ended up empty on the side of Bell Road about three weeks ago."

My eyes filled as I struggled to gain control of my fear. "Guys, this is police stuff, maybe FBI. Uh, SWAT teams and whoever. Going after hijackers at night is like swimming with sharks when your leg's bleeding."

"Not quite," replied Mike. "Because in this case, we know exactly how many sharks and what they look like." Then he pulled something from his back pocket. "Plus we've got a name for one of them."

I spilled coffee on my ankles. "How? What?"

He held it by the edges. "I took the driver's license off the guard after I calmed him down."

"Calmed him down?" I sputtered. "You practically killed him with your fists."

"Don't exaggerate. I just broke his ankle so he'd be out of the mix."

Eric leaned close enough to peer at the ID. "I think y'all might've skipped a few details."

"I-I'm going back inside," I said, with a knot in my throat. "Can't listen to this." And I left.

Still attired as she was when she'd brought out the coffee, Velma sat in front of the television but seemed to have her ear on the porch conversation. "Sounds like they're gonna go howl at the moon."

"Velma, this isn't about carousing with buddies." I crouched down by her chair and lowered my voice as I tried to steady it. "Those hijackers killed a man and most likely intended the same for us. We have to leave this matter to law enforcement."

"What about that medicine in your cousin's duffle bag?"

"I know, it complicates things."

"You probably don't have a record, Tricia, so maybe

you'd get off with probation if cops find drugs in your car." Velma smoothed the front of her apron. "But I know lots of girls who went to jail because their boyfriends or husbands couldn't keep off drugs." She nodded. "Cops don't care whether you even knew it was there. If you're close enough to hit it with a broom, you're an accessory."

She was probably right. No, I didn't have a record, and didn't want to start one, either. "So you're willing to sit here and let them go chase after dangerous criminals?"

"Not exactly," replied Velma, as she clicked off the TV remote, stood slowly, and stretched her voluptuous figure. "We'd better go along and try to keep them out of trouble."

9

Monday, 12:05 a.m.

My jaw dropped open but no words fell out.

Velma eyed me up and down, torn clothing, bush-slashed arms, cut face, and all. "We better get you dressed," she said calmly. "Looks like we're going operational." Then she pursed her lips. "My stuff won't fit you too good, but it'll do. The main thing is shoes."

"Huh?" I was still dazed that these lunatics were about to embark on a dangerous mission and Velma the stripper was discussing footwear.

"I can probably put you in either boots or running shoes. But you'll have to wear two pairs of socks." She rolled her eyes. "I'm a tight eight."

I was too, but had no intention of admitting it.

About ten minutes later I emerged from her closet looking better than when I had arrived—since the replacement clothes were not soiled or torn—but Velma's garments hung quite loose on my less voluptuous bust and hips.

"Ready?" asked Velma, looking toasty warm in a long cowgirl duster. She handed me a sandwich. "I expect we'll be leaving soon. Some of these missions take two or three hours."

"You've done this before?"

"Couple of times." She pointed toward the porch. "Eric and his buddies had gone on several of these vigilante runs and I was suspicious they were just hanging out at a bar or finding some other trouble, so I told him he couldn't go without me."

"What did he say to that?"

"He gave me a big hug and said it was great to have hobbies we could share."

"Hobbies? Vigilante runs?" *What kind of bizarre world is Marrowbone, anyway?*

I took a bite. Cold bologna and cheese on plain white bread. No mayo. It was clear her culinary skills were not the attributes which had captivated Eric's devotion. Not my current concern. Taking my meager meal into the living room, I caught the tail end of Mike's and Eric's high-level porch planning.

"...and my buddy down the road has the wrecker. Already called him and he's good to go. We'll pick up three more guys at the blinking light."

I whipped open the screen door and stomped out to the porch. "You guys are crazy if you think we're all going to load up and chase down those, those pirates!" I started sobbing. "It's... it's..."

"Settle down, Tricia," said Mike as he hugged me. "Sure, hijackers are dangerous, but there's only six and one's already down with a busted ankle. Besides, these guys are also vulnerable."

"Vulnerable, how?" I blubbered.

"At least one of the others didn't know what he was doing." Mike tried to use a warm soothing voice, but the words felt like jagged slivers of ice in my ears. "And from the way those other three mishandled that cargo, I'm guessing this was their first job."

Eric weighed in. "Two small trucks with little trailers is the giveaway—amateurs."

"The leader of those amateurs killed the driver." I struggled to hold back my sobs.

"I'm not pretending they're saints. Just saying I don't think they're pros." He nodded in Eric's direction. "So it should be a lot easier to outmaneuver them."

"What about Mr. Big?" I said in a flat tone. "He's definitely been around the block before."

"True... true," replied Mike. "And basically, he's the main one we really have to worry about." He cocked an eyebrow at Eric. "Got an extra gun to loan me? Mr. Big stole my revolver."

Eric nodded. "Yeah, I can loan you pretty much any caliber except a Sharps buffalo gun."

"What I normally carry is a .357."

"Got just the one for you," said Eric. "It's a Smith & Wesson Model 686. Stainless... six-inch barrel."

"Perfect. In fact..."

"We're going, too," I interrupted, my own ears not believing my words.

"If you come," said Mike, "you've got to stay in the wrecker."

"Velma, too?"

"Velma's operational," replied Eric. "She's our official distraction."

"Going after dangerous criminals, you certainly don't need any distractions," I said, trying to waggle my shaking finger.

"Not for us," said Eric, grinning broadly. "She distracts the bad guys." Offering no further explanation, he turned to Mike. "What did you call the main deal?"

"Standard envelopment," replied Mike.

"Yeah, this is a new twist on the Marrowbone Method," explained Eric. "Usually we just run in shooting and yelling... and the bad guys are too scared to move."

"If we work this envelopment maneuver properly," added Mike, "we won't even need to shoot anybody."

"So why the guns?" I asked.

"In case we have to," responded Eric. "Duh."

They spoke of possibly shooting some murdering hijackers as though it were changing a tire.

Mike gazed into my worried face. "What's wrong?"

I swallowed a sandwich bite I'd neglected to chew. "What makes you think these guys are still hanging around?"

He reached a muscular arm around my shoulders. "If they're gone, we abort the capture part of our mission. We mainly want your car and my duffle." His calm voice was presumably designed to be consoling. "But they won't be gone, Tricia, because they know we're witnesses."

Not only battered and exhausted, but now I was outvoted in a sudden, life-altering election. *Why wouldn't they listen to reason?* I slumped over in resignation and stared at my feet in Velma's shoes. "At least give me a different gun." I carefully pulled the guard's pistol out of my purse, released the magazine, pulled back the slide, and handed everything to Mike. "Don't like these semi-autos. You never know whether they're cocked and locked... or not."

Grinning broadly, Eric reached into his back pocket. "I've got just the gun for you—Smith Model 60, Chief's Special." He pointed the muzzle away and opened the cylinder to show it was loaded, then held it by the top strap, so the cylinder couldn't close. "It's a .38, Tricia. Hardly any kick at all."

I reached for it, pointed the muzzle away, and closed up the cylinder. I'd handled plenty of revolvers. "Thanks. Anything to carry it in?"

"I've got a little belt clip holster that fits it," Eric replied. "You got a belt?"

Velma disappeared back inside the house and re-emerged with a gaudy leather belt, which I needed anyway since my hips didn't hold up her jeans.

"Okay, all situated?" asked Mike.

I swallowed the last bite of my dry sandwich, plopped down on the porch steps, and carefully placed the gun beside me. "I can't believe I'm the only one who hopes the bad guys are gone." I pointed toward the nearly full moon. "It's the middle of the night, I can barely keep my eyes open, and I hurt all over. Instead of heading safely home, I'm part of some Wild West round-up of cattle rustlers. How can I possibly drag myself to work and once again rescue Mr. Dross' hide—in hardly nine hours?"

"Okay, things are gearing up, Tricia. Which part confuses you the most?"

10

12:26 a.m.

I paused by Eric's crew cab pickup. Mike had draped his long arm across my trembling shoulders and made it seem almost plausible that, to regain my busted car and his medicinal duffle, we should charge five dangerous hijackers with a gaggle of armed lunatics and an ex-stripper.

Of course he never satisfactorily explained the *how* of this operation… or his blind certainty things could possibly end well. My default setting is to extra-plan and over-schedule and then continue to worry things will disintegrate. Mike acted like his M.O. of jumping in and swinging fists was the proper homeopathic approach to life's problems.

"Eric," I asked, "what on earth are we doing?"

With a loud grunt, he opened the truck's door for me. "You've known me a long time, haven't you?"

I nodded. "Maybe a dozen years or so."

"During that time, have I ever steered you wrong?"

It was a trick question, because I had never been steered

anywhere by Eric. "Well, you remind me of the character Tom Jones," I said finally. "Jumping from one adventure to another, having a series of near misses, but somehow always managing to come out on top."

"I am what I am," he said without blinking. With less of his middle Tennessee accent, he could have been Popeye the Sailor. "Good instincts and lots of luck."

"Yes, Eric, you're usually lucky... but are you always right?"

"What we're doing tonight is right."

"But would you involve yourself if you didn't know one of the victims?"

His reply contained no actual answer. "Tricia, things aren't nearly as complicated as you women want to make them."

I gave up and climbed in. We headed out.

Our main force met the dark-skinned wrecker guy down the road, paused long enough to ensure he was armed and sober, and then we five convoyed to Marrowbone's unblinking blinking traffic light to collect the other three vigilantes in two more trucks. Didn't recognize any of them from school in Verdeville, so I figured they'd later gravitated to Eric under other circumstances, like work or community.

A surge of adrenaline shook me and I squinted, trying to make out the new guys in the darkness of the corner's empty parking lot. I'd been introduced to the four new vigilantes, each in his twenties or thirties, but in my stasis of stunned fear, I'd registered no names. They were hardly more than dark silhouettes under the glaring curb light where we'd assembled. So I tagged them Wrecker, Skinny, Baldy, and Hippie. I chose the latter nickname not because of his personality or unnoticeable hips... but simply due to the long stringy hair.

"Velma, I've got to ask. Aren't you the least bit afraid of distracting—whatever that means—those dangerous bad guys?"

She looked at me in all seriousness and said, "You can't be any safer than when you're escorted by five Marrowbone men carrying ten guns. The only way I'll get hurt is if I trip on a rock or step in a pothole." Then she sighed languidly. "Besides, and this is no secret to Eric—I'm an exhalationist."

I figured she meant exhibitionist, but it was not the time for grammar lessons. Seemed exponentially naïve to me— whatever she had planned with that duster—but if I had her body, maybe I'd distract armed criminals while my colleagues pounced on them. *When pigs fly.* I was terrified. Figured I'd be lucky to survive cowering in one of the truck cabs.

Finally, everyone was loaded in four vehicles. The West Team—Baldy, Wrecker, and me in the wrecker, plus Mike with Eric in Eric's truck—left ten minutes early. Skinny and Hippie—with whom Mike had a short, private chat—were on the East Team with the distracting Velma. They had two trucks among them.

Wrecker, the man, was affable enough. However, I could tell by the expression on his coffee-colored face he was on edge. Baldy seemed relatively serene, which made me suspect he had only marginal awareness of what we were heading into… or had smoked a funny cigarette.

Between Wrecker and Baldy and their two guns apiece, in the middle of the otherwise spacious cab, I couldn't get comfortable. I hoped and prayed the bad guys would be long gone. Otherwise, I'd have my head tucked between my knees and my hands over my ears.

11

It took our West Team roughly twenty minutes to drive the four miles south, thirteen miles west on I-40, and then about three miles north again to circle around the back side of where we'd left my car just outside Hermitage.

Earlier, I hadn't realized the highway stretch where my car had died was on a fairly pronounced curve. As our two vehicles approached, Eric's truck (conveying him and Mike) pulled over just before the wrecker carrying me rounded the curve. Obviously they wanted our vehicles to remain out of sight of anyone who might be near my stranded sedan or the big rig, which had been eased up 'til it was within a few feet of my Toyota's rear bumper. It was puzzling they'd seen fit to move the eighteen-wheeler about a mile, but not to drive it away somewhere else. I could only assume that signaled the hijackers' intention to have further dealings with the truck, my car, and whoever returned to get either one. My guess caused a bonfire of fear in my guts.

It was 12:58 a.m.

Our headlights were out, of course, but there was sufficient moonlight to watch Mike and Eric leap from his truck and scurry up the south shoulder 'til they reached a spot where they could better see around the curve. When Baldy and Wrecker also jumped out of our cab, I did, too, but a diligent Wrecker waved me back.

"You're supposed to stay in the truck," he whispered hoarsely.

"No way I'm hanging back here while all you guys are up there somewhere." I'd seen movies where the pretty girl stays alone in a truck and gets mauled by the zombies. I wasn't claiming to be a beauty queen, but figured I was at least attractive enough to entice the local ghouls.

"Eric's gonna be mad."

"Tough toenails. He can turn me in to the principal."

Wrecker gave me an odd look, then grinned (showing gleaming white teeth) and hunkered over, trotting toward the others up ahead. When I caught up, they were all down in a dry concrete culvert thing stretching beneath the highway, which I guessed channeled runoff water between the ditches that paralleled the road, north and south. It gave us a good vantage point and we couldn't be seen by anyone near the two vehicles ahead—if, indeed, anyone was still there.

Eric ignored my unexpected appearance, but Mike hugged me sideways while keeping his eyes on the enemy site ahead.

"Just like I figured," hissed Eric.

I couldn't see much of anything. "What?"

"They're all gone," he replied. "Probably hauling those choppers to Memphis or Chattanooga by now."

Mike poked his upper arm. "Not everybody." He

pointed east. "Mr. Big posted a guard."

"One guy," said Eric, squinting. "Guess he figured you'd be back for the car."

The trunk lid was still closed, as best I could tell peering around the immense bulk of the tractor-trailer. So presumably Mike's stash was intact unless they'd sniffed it out.

"He doesn't want to lose track of the witnesses," said Mike quietly.

Neither Baldy nor Wrecker added anything. Each kept one of their guns pointed forward and both appeared reasonably calm under the dangerous circumstances. At least settled enough to suggest they'd been on these junkets before and were used to waiting and watching in the dark.

I wasn't. My impulse was to chatter. So I tugged on Mike's sleeve. "With only one man on watch, we can, uh, stand down this mission. No reason to put Velma in jeopardy and nobody needs to get himself shot." Not sure where that came from. What I was thinking was how much I'd rather be in Marrowbone… if not completely back to Verdeville.

Eric answered first. "Uh, I don't think…"

"The show's over," my nerves interrupted him. "Two of our armed guys in one truck can drive up there, buffalo the guard, he'll turn tail, and we get my car back."

"Not that simple, Tricia." Eric didn't take his eyes off the back of the rig.

I kept tugging on Mike's shirt.

"Mr. Big and those other three guys are coming back," he said. "Bank on it."

He was counting out Sentry, whose ankle he'd broken a few hours ago. I exhaled heavily. "Then let's hurry. Drive in, scare him off, and get my car."

"Can't rush this." Mike stared straight ahead. "Everything's not always what it seems."

I turned around and leaned my back against the culvert's cold concrete. "Don't borrow trouble, Mike. We lucked into perfect timing. Let's grab my car before those other creeps get back."

No response from either Baldy or Wrecker, though the latter appraised me like he approved of my plan. Remaining silent, Eric waited for Mike's reaction.

Mike reared back his head and sniffed the air, like he'd done in the woods some hours before. "I don't think that guard's alone. Somebody else is out there."

Eric whipped his eyes forward again. "Where?"

"Most likely in the back of that big rig." Mike pointed, but it's pointless to point in the dark. "He's probably playing solitaire and sipping coffee."

"And waiting for us," added Eric.

This was a setback in my sunny assessment, but I continued to press for a hasty resolution. "So, two total. We send three guys to take them out and we get my car."

"Maybe two," said Mike. "Might be…"

I remembered something and clutched Mike's arm again. "Everything keeps changing. We need to contact Velma so she won't start whatever her distractions are."

"Can't," replied Mike. "We can't signal her without giving away our presence and position."

Eric leaned closer. "It's on the clock, Tricia. Velma takes off down the highway at 1:07."

Disgusted—and profusely sweating my anxiety—I slumped again with my back to the rough concrete. "Well, we're going to be throwing a mighty big party for one lone guy watching my car and a big *maybe* who could be hiding in the trailer."

"When facing hijackers at night, other things being equal," intoned Mike, as though he'd worked this same operation a dozen times, "I'd much rather be positive I had more men and we all carried bigger guns with more ammo."

Eric checked his watch. "Three minutes 'til show time. Let's get in position."

"Wait, guys." I was surprised to discover tears again welling in my eyes. "Cancel the mission. Leave the car. I'll report it stolen and maybe get a better one with the insurance."

"Too late," said Mike. "This is green light."

"It's *my* car," I said, my eyes burning.

"True, but it contains some of my property," Mike whispered. "Besides, we're here and ready to engage."

I felt like screaming or slugging somebody, but either one would blow our stealth.

"You stay back here, Tricia, and keep low." Mike gripped my shoulder.

"One more quick run-through of the plan," said Eric.

Mike nodded and the other two guys leaned in. "When we get a little closer, we split up, me to the north side and Eric to the south. You two," he jabbed the chests of Wrecker and Baldy, "split up also. One on me and one on Eric." Wrecker moved closer to Eric, so that left Baldy with Mike. "All of us head east at the same time, we sneak up to the eighteen-wheeler, and you two south guys check the back of the rig for any other hijackers."

"If anybody's in the back, we'll take them out," said Eric.

"Good. Then we all keep moving toward the guard at the front of the truck... but don't get all the way behind him in case somebody has to shoot."

"Nope, don't want a crossfire," replied Eric. "We never

do crossfires in Marrowbone."

"With luck, he won't even see you 'til you conk him on the head."

"In your, um, classic envelopment, Mike, what do you usually conk with?"

Mike replied like a long-tenured college lecturer. "This is more of a modified envelopment, so it doesn't matter. Weapon of choice."

"I'd rather a baseball bat for conking," Eric said, "but a gun barrel's okay, too."

"Go for it." Mike seemed distracted. He sniffed the air again.

"You just want him out... right?" asked Eric. "Not dead."

"Out is sufficient."

"So you're not worried he'll ID us to the cops when they question him?" I asked.

"He doesn't know anybody's names," answered Mike. "Any other questions?"

Baldy shook his bare scalp and Wrecker mumbled, "Nah."

"Yeah... mine," I said. "I saw you talking to Hippie before we took off."

"Which one's Hippie?" asked Mike.

"Long hair," I said, leveling my hand at my shoulder top. "So what did you tell him?"

Eric leaned closer. "I was wondering that, too."

Without taking his eyes off the targets ahead, Mike replied, "On top of his Velma escort, I just gave him a special assignment."

Eric shrugged and eyed the time again. "Ready?"

Mike flexed his hands. "Let's roll."

12

Didn't like it one bit, but I followed instructions and stayed back in the culvert as Mike, Eric, Wrecker, and Baldy split into two pairs and crept along the rough gravel of their respective shoulders. At that stretch, the highway's curve gave them plenty of cover. And the nearby woods were dense, as I well remembered from our earlier frantic foray.

Either the East Team had started late or Velma was walking slowly, because it was already 1:13 a.m. and there were no sounds or lights from the area around my car and the big rig. Since I'd missed part of the hurried planning session back at Eric's place, I wasn't certain what to expect but assumed Velma would draw attention to herself in a way obvious enough that she'd be readily seen but not fired upon. No doubt she'd practiced something with that duster. Presumably it would focus the guard's eyes east and our team could get close.

The two pairs in West Team had scurried so far around

the curve that I could no longer spot them, so I exited the culvert. Whatever was going to happen, at least I needed to *see* it… even if I had to close my eyes. So I crossed the highway in a low crouching run like I recalled from the war movies I'd watched with my dad. Out of breath, I dropped onto the slope between the highway's graveled shoulder and the ditch on its north side.

Finally I spotted Velma, a long way off. She'd solved the visibility issue by holding a camp lantern over her head. Her buttoned and belted duster swayed with her steps, a shapeless shadow behind her mobile hips where the little light didn't reach. If anyone expected *that* distraction to turn the guard's head… he'd more likely shoot her, and my throat clenched at the thought.

Couldn't actually see the hijacker guard, but I noticed movement between my car and the cab of the big rig.

As Velma got closer, I could see more details. Her duster was buttoned at the top but the bottom was loose. Its sides flapped as she walked, revealing her shapely bare legs with each step. When she finally got within about forty feet, she began chatting loudly with the guard. Though I was too far away to hear their actual dialog, from the way she waggled her hips and eased open the duster's belt, her words didn't matter. Her goal was to keep him interested and imply he'd soon see more of her. I knew Skinny and Hippie were supposed to be on her flanks, most likely in the ditches which straddled the highway, but the darkness and slope and curve concealed them.

I'd again lost sight of my four fellow West Teamers, but figured they were up ahead — two on either road shoulder, all ready to pounce on the guard and whoever might be in the rig. I rose to my knees for a better look.

Velma gave me one. When she got within twenty feet of the sentry, she stopped, whipped open the duster, and waggled the flashlight beam over her ample front. Color shimmered and blazed in the sharp finger of light... neon orange with spangles, a shade so bright it could burn retinas all the way to Marrowbone. A tiny bit of orange bikini to corral a whole lot of flesh. Then she coyly draped half of the duster back into place, cleavage visible above the lowered lapel on the other side, still lit up.

Distraction—perfect. No Tennessee male would shoot that target. With the guard's total attention on Velma's optic orange attributes, three West Teamers and one East Teamer from the ditch converged on him.

The guard went down like a sack of horse feed dropped from a loading dock.

Velma extinguished her light, clutched her duster tightly, darted to the shoulder beside the big rig, and lit a cigarette.

After securing the unconscious guard, the four good guys moved toward my car. The other East Teamer was not visible from my distant vantage point and all of our party were only dark shapes in the moonlight.

Assuming everything had gone according to plan, I was about to jump up and trot toward the gathering when the hair on the back of my neck prickled like I'd touched a live circuit. Something was wrong. Not just that two of our guys were unaccounted for, either. It was as though I were able to sniff the air, as I'd seen Mike do, and discern some important detail from the breeze. Eerie.

About a hundred feet west of the eighteen-wheeler, I dropped down flat to the rough gravel of the north shoulder and strained to examine the dark scene before me.

Bright lights suddenly flashed on and swept back and

forth. Voices yelled from the north and south woods.

Ambush! My throat instinctively wanted to scream, but I bit hard on my lip and tried to fight down the panic. Terrified, I slid over 'til the north slope mostly hid my prone body.

No firing yet. But chaos ensued. The four good guys whipped into a defensive barrier around Velma, against the rig's four huge driver-side wheels, and faced outward, guns ready. From the woods, Mr. Big shouted—bullying and incoherent words that seemed to echo on nothing. Light beams zoomed about like bright fingers unsettled in the night. And handguns waggled, the good guys' aim yanking nervously about as if trying to follow the shouts.

I could picture eight or nine sweaty trigger fingers not knowing what to do. Shooting would likely commence when the shouting stopped. It was only a matter of time. And then... with all those guns around? Someone would probably die.

My heart contracted. It pounded so loud, I could barely hear the din up ahead. I crept closer along the grassy slope. My presence was no good to anybody that far back, so I had to get closer and figure out a way to help... without getting myself killed in the process. Needed to figure out where the other two good guys were. Had to do something or scream. *Where are your night vision goggles when you need them?*

It didn't take a genius to realize the spotlights were held by Mr. Big and company. No telling how long they'd waited in the woods for us to come back for my car. I wondered if they were surprised at how many had showed up.

One light went off. "Turn off those lights," commanded Mr. Big's voice, suddenly clear, and the three remaining beams went dark in staggered sequence.

In the moonlight, Mr. Big and one thug emerged cautiously from the north side woods. Two others appeared from the south side, crouched over, and ran toward the truck—one curling around the front and the other skirting the back. All had guns, and at that close range, a bullet's a bullet and all can kill, no matter the caliber.

Ignoring Mr. Big's booming voice yelling threats and orders, I scurried closer along the north shoulder's slope, almost down in the ditch. My sole advantage—no one, good guys or bad, was expecting me. One huddled body was down on the pavement edge of the north shoulder, not too far ahead of me. From the moonlight's reflection on his pale noggin, it had to be Baldy. Wasn't sure when he got hit or by whom—or how badly he was injured—but Baldy was not moving. I'd only known him for an hour or so. That wasn't enough time. I prayed he was still alive.

Shapes and profiles were difficult to distinguish in the darkness. But of the four good guys still standing, it looked like Mike and Eric braced shoulder to shoulder in front of Velma, guns raised and facing the enemy to the north. On either side of them were Wrecker and Skinny, facing east and west. No one could sneak up on their flanks from around the truck without attracting some hostile attention.

That left only Hippie, from Velma's distraction team, who had evidently hung back on the east end, most likely somewhere in the north ditch. I wondered if that was what Mike had indicated in his private, last minute briefing.

Mr. Big continued to spout off his threats, punctuated by vile curses. I kept ignoring him, even though his voice made my heart hammer ever faster. He'd claimed I was his property. He had more guns. Every nerve I had screamed at me to run and hide. But I couldn't.

Baldy's pate glimmered. Though not moving, it looked as though he was still breathing. Again I fought the instinct to flee. I could only manage one forward inch at a time. Those inches were the hardest I'd ever moved in my life.

I'd seen plenty of movie standoffs, but this was my first real-life encounter. Terrifying. *You figure at any second, somebody's trigger finger twitches and then a dozen guns start blazing.* My gut burned and my knees already ached from crawling. Each reluctant movement brought me closer to Mr. Big's running monologue. Still holding his position, laying low against the grassy north slope, Mr. Big demanded surrender. *If they do, we're all dead.* Mike, speaking for the good guys with eight loaded weapons, insisted the opposite.

They were pretty evenly matched, but the enemy had lots of cover. Our Marrowbone Marauders were in the open, only their backs covered by the eighteen wheeler.

And there I was with a borrowed popgun, creeping up along the north slope toward Mr. Big. Hippie was somewhere out there, presumably still functional and hopefully approaching from the opposite end. I'd heard Eric say something about crossfires, and it appeared Hippie and I might be accidentally setting one up. No way of notifying the other party.

Mike had said the hijacker minions seemed like amateurs who'd scatter if their leader went down, so I figured the best thing was to focus on Mr. Big. But how could I communicate with Mike?

What happened next was totally bizarre. As my brain stressed over the distance between us, I had a flashback of Mike rearing back his head and sniffing the air—first in the woods and later on the roadside. Whatever it was, something about Mike could discern data which regular humans didn't or couldn't sense. Just thinking about it made me squirm inside. But I had to do something to let the good guys know what I was doing, and trusting Mike's offbeat abilities was my only hope.

I shut my eyes and said to myself, "Mike, I'm on the north slope, crawling east." Zap! The second I raised my head and opened my eyes, Mike whipped around and stared directly toward me... even though he could not possibly have known where I was.

Weird... a telepathic connection. A real one.

I crawled a few more agonizing feet and stopped for a breath. Mike eyed my exact position. A few more feet and another pause. Surely he couldn't actually *see* me on that slope across the highway, but he looked in my precise direction each time I checked. And he seemed intuitively to know not only where I was but what I was doing. Unfortunately, all that telepathy traveled only in one direction, because I had no stinking clue what he was thinking or planning, or when he intended to launch it.

Mike whispered something to Eric, who relayed it to Velma, who (in turn) whispered to Wrecker and Skinny. At least all five of *them* were on one page. *Wish I knew...*

Hippie was totally out of the loop, too. Whatever else happened tonight, I did *not* want to be felled by friendly fire. I could only hope Hippie was perceptive, alert, and ready to move. Whenever and wherever.

But what? Our envelopment had been enveloped... or ambushed, anyway. Velma's elaborate distraction had been wasted on the single guard. *What do they call a maneuver to outmaneuver the bad guys who've ambushed our envelopment?* Suddenly it came to me—I was the sniper!

13

There I was, at 1:20 a.m., without my car, in deadly peril—the worst prepared, least experienced, most terrified member of the ad hoc Marrowbone Marauders, and I'd been *de facto* elected sniper to take out the enemy leader. In the dark. With a five-shot snubby .38.

I wasn't worried about my gun handling in general. On a range, with ear and eye protection, I could drive tacks into paper targets at twenty-one feet. But to shoot a living, moving human target, at thirty feet or more... with my hands trembling? The thought was enough to make them shake harder.

Hippie could be twenty feet from me and have me in his sights, and I wouldn't know it. Which gave me an idea. If I couldn't see much of anything along this shadowy slope, neither could Mr. Big and his thugs. So I should be able to close the distance without being spotted. Especially since they apparently thought they'd ambushed our entire squad.

Each time Mike turned in my direction, his eyes found me, spot on. And that link created enough electricity to make my hair stand on end. I shivered at the jolt, swallowed hard, and kept crawling.

Then I paused and thought again. When I got closer, I wouldn't be able to stay on that slope without being seen. Traipsing through the woods toward the thugs would make too much noise—not to mention I couldn't stand tussling again with spiders and briars. No, I needed to be lower. Maybe I should crawl along the lowest part of the ditch.

One last check on the five besieged Marrowbone Marauders, and they were all where they'd been before. I wondered why they hadn't taken cover in the clearance beneath the cab.

Even in the dark, the slight shake of Mike's head was unmistakable. And suddenly I didn't need to hear his voice to understand. If the Marauders dropped and started crawling for cover, at least one of the criminals would surely open fire, with or without Mr. Big's orders. If the standoff lurched further into crisis mode, someone would die.

So they were trapped in the open until somebody else did something. Me.

I slid down into the ditch. Thankfully it hadn't rained too recently and the grassy bottom was merely semi-dry mud. Started to crawl on my belly. *Velma will kill me when she sees how I've wrecked her clothes.*

But the feel of it made me shudder. Couldn't belly crawl—way too icky. I had to use an odd sort of slither on my elbows and knees... and it must've looked really ugly. Fortunately, the ditch was deep enough that my butt couldn't be seen above the edges.

Slowly made my ungainly way along the ditch toward

Mr. Big. More vile and blustery chatter from him, but neither Mike nor Eric responded. I wanted to pause and scramble up the slope where I could see if the Marrowbone Five were any closer to making a move. Too dangerous, though. I knew Mike's telepathic eyes were fixed directly on my position.

Their classic, terrifying standoff continued. Lots of guys with plenty of ammo and nobody truly wanting to shoot first, because they'd be mowed down by return fire. Nobody willing to lay down their guns, either. In movies, it was often the good guys putting down weapons and then the evil bunch commencing torture, rape, and murder. Every time I'd seen that in films, I'd screamed—though usually to myself—*don't be stupid, good guys... they'll never let you live!* I could only hope Mike and Eric had viewed those same movies.

My brain pounded with fear as my sweaty body maneuvered along that nasty ditch bottom. I'd lost track of the military terms, but apparently I was about to ambush the guys who'd trapped our envelopment, after our distraction had been compromised.

Made it to about thirty feet from Mr. Big—still outside my most accurate shooting range. I raised up from the ditch bottom and peeked out one last time. But my elevation was way too low. Couldn't see anything of the good guys from there, so I'd have to crawl back up the slope.

Moving inch by slow inch and melting into the cool grass, I silently made my way high enough to check my team once again. Mike spotted me immediately. Another whispered exchange among the Marrowbones. Then Mike and Eric parted slightly and slowly, as if reluctant, and Velma wriggled from between them.

"Since you guys just want to talk, I'm gonna liven things up a bit," she said, loud enough for Mr. Big to hear, but with a soft, breathy quality she'd apparently borrowed from the late Marilyn Monroe. "I used to be a professional exotic dancer," she ran her hands down her curvy hips, "and I know some moves you slugs have probably never seen." She shrugged one toned arm out of the duster's sleeve, the coat itself grasped up around her neck.

Astonishing. Nine armed rednecks and I were about to watch a stripper on the side of Highway 70, just outside Hermitage. If that had taken place in Greene County, it could've been a minor scandal. But on the eastern fringe of Davidson County, possibly it was commonplace. Instead of returning to the ditch I instinctively kept crawling on the slope. With all the attention on Velma, nobody would be looking in my direction anyhow.

"Now, I spent a lot of money on this costume, with all these reflective spangles," she continued, in her hypnotic voice and with gentle swaying of her shapely hips. "So the least you guys can do is give me a spotlight or two. You won't get the full effect if I take this off in the dark."

It was bold and brassy. Velma was fearless… or maybe she was such an *exhalationist* that showing off her body really was as natural to her as breathing.

She shrugged her other arm from the second sleeve but kept the duster strategically positioned. "So who's got that spotlight?"

"Maybe you're wearing your grandma's housedress under that coat, lady," yelled the thug next to Mr. Big.

"Shut up! She's just playing you."

Evidently, tucked into the woods as they'd been, the bad guys hadn't seen Velma's bold strides down the middle of the highway with her swaying duster, nor her approach to the erstwhile guard, the orange teeny bikini reflecting moonlight and the lantern she'd started out with. But I'd certainly never forget it.

"This ain't no housedress, cowboy," said Velma, as she expertly flashed one side of the duster and gave an instant eyeful to the two north slope hijackers. "Now, give me some light and I think we've got time for a quick show before you guys start killing each other."

Probably sounded logical to all parties. In fact, if I'd been born male, I figure I would've sat up and stared, not wanting to miss a nanosecond of Velma's performance. *But I'm not a guy.* A full-grown, formerly structured and orderly woman, I'd been crawling on my elbows and knees through a nasty ditch in the middle of the night, when I should've been home in Verdeville sleeping comfortably. I ducked back down and kept crawling on my belly along the slope.

Closer. Within fifteen feet of Mr. Big and he still had not spotted me. I stopped again, propped my wrists on a clump which I hoped was not an ant pile, and double-fisted my snubby revolver with the front ramp blade on Mr. Big's right shoulder. This would be an easier shot if he was facing me, so I knew there was a chance I could miss. But I figured to spread my shots and, even if he lurched, at least one of the five should hit some piece of him.

I couldn't afford to shift my gaze to the Marrowbone Five at my right, but out of the corner of my eye, a flashlight beam shone on the dazzling optic orange bikini as Velma suddenly and seductively dropped her duster to the shoulder's packed gravel.

Her voluptuous body, nude except for the teeny bikini, was the obvious signal and at 1:35 a.m. everything happened at once.

Recoil and gunpowder smell were the same as firing at a range, but without ear protection the noise was painfully stunning. I fired at Mr. Big, who bolted like a frantic squirrel and shot back wildly in my general direction. Though my belly had been churning with heated lava through much of the past half hour, it now turned to ice as I realized his bullets were aimed at me!

Mike and Eric thrust Velma to the ground and then rolled her back toward the four huge wheels behind them. The flashlight went out and somebody—presumably Hippie, judging from the direction—shot at the thug who'd been holding it. Skinny and Wrecker slid over and crouched in front of Velma's prone body, shielding her. Mike and Eric— quickly separated by some dozen feet—tore across the highway toward Mr. Big.

Velma was secure. Wrecker went after the two south slope hijackers, who had retreated into the dark, dense woods.

I couldn't find my target any more, so I tumbled down the slope and tried to melt into the side of the ditch. Bullets were flying. Mr. Big shot toward Mike and Eric, and they both fired back. The flashlight guy was silent. Maybe Hippie had nailed him.

It all seemed to play out in super slo-mo. But it only took seconds.

The shooting stopped. Eric and Mike crouched low at the edge of the north woods. Eric hovered over the flashlight guy, who huddled in a writhing lump. Eric disarmed him and conked him on the head, ending his portion of the party.

Back up on road level, Skinny continued to protect Velma. Wrecker kept chasing after the two runners.

So where was Mr. Big?

I must have missed him completely, so my single shot did little besides igniting the fusillade. But I had four more cartridges in this snubby and full intention of using every one if necessary. We'd come too far and done too much to end this night with Mr. Big getting away scot-free.

Movement behind me in the ditch. I whipped around and stared into the cavernous muzzle of Mr. Big's .45 caliber semi-auto pistol.

14

It's a different type of standoff when you're holding one of the guns. My guts iced over and my arms trembled. I held onto the revolver with both hands and thumbed back the hammer.

His looks were as lacking as his charm. "So you're the pitiful ace they hid up their sleeve," said Mr. Big breathlessly. He was evidently not used to scurrying through woods and dodging bullets. Perhaps he was more a white collar hijacker. "Well, it looks like I've captured their queen."

He'd wrecked his own imagery, but my brain couldn't focus on that. Maybe I should have said something clever or tried to sound brave, but considering how close I was to blubbering, I just kept my mouth shut and shook my head slowly. I also lowered my aim to his mid-torso, so I could not possibly miss at seven feet.

"My crew wanted to take all those choppers and go, but I knew you idiots would come back." More heavy breathing and he glanced left then right. "Took you a lot longer than I'd figured, though. We nearly gave up."

"If you'd left us alone," I said, finally locating my shaky voice, "we'd be gone and so would you."

"But I couldn't let two loose ends hang on my otherwise clean job."

"Not so clean. You killed the driver."

"That was his own suicide," retorted Big. "I told him to drop his gun."

"No, it's lethal injection in this state. It's you strapped on a gurney…"

"No, 'fraid not, lady. You see, now I have a hostage."

"Then you'll have at least one hole in your belly and still have to carry me."

"Oh, you think this is like Hollywood?" He looked aside abruptly, as though he'd heard something, then turned back. "Well, in real life things work different." Crouching, he took a half step.

I didn't know this in the sense of rational knowledge, but my instinct screamed, "Don't let him get any closer," so I squeezed the trigger.

The muzzle flash temporarily blinded me and the report assaulted my ears. No other shots except Mr. Big's flash and answering boom, immediately after mine. In that second, I was certain I'd hit him and terrified he might've hit me. But no time to check for bullet holes.

Before my ears stopped ringing, Mike zoomed over me and smashed Mr. Big in the chest. Both tumbled into the ditch. Fists flew—four or five vicious blows. Then Mike knelt beside a limp body. He stripped away Big's weapons, including his own revolver. He tossed the hijacker's semi-auto onto the highway shoulder and hurried over.

I struggled to sit up. My ears still rang and my eyes began pouring.

"Are you okay, Tricia?" asked Mike. He hugged me tightly.

I nodded, but my voice was gone. Something wet and dark covered his neck and shoulder. My breath caught and I pointed.

But Mike shook his head. "That's Mr. Big's blood. You tagged him."

I cleared my throat and wiped my eyes. "Is he dead?"

"Not even close. You nicked his left armpit. What were you aiming at?"

"Just above his belly button."

"Well, I guess you're anticipating the recoil. That pulls your aim right and up a bit."

"Next time I shoot a hijacker at night, I'll try to remember that." Then I hugged him so tightly I temporarily forgot he was a twice-removed third cousin-in-law.

With my eyes dried, I glanced around. Eric started toward us, but I waved him toward the huddled form in the grass, its bald head reflecting the moonlight. I'd crawled right past him but hadn't had time even to check.

Skinny held Velma's duster for her, helped her to a seat on the big rig's steps, then stood guard beside her. "Don't touch anything," he said.

Wrecker and Hippie emerged from the line of underbrush bordering the south woods.

"Those guys are gone," Wrecker said, speaking of the thugs who'd taken off running. "They're probably at I-40 by now."

Surely that was a gross exaggeration. Six miles of heavy woods…

"One got away," said Hippie, pointing over his shoulder and nearly out of breath. "I found a logging road and heard some vehicle take off. Left behind two pickups with empty trailers."

"Let's tie up these punks and get going," said Mike as he disengaged.

I tried—really I did—but couldn't seem to get my footing and I collapsed back into the semi-dry mud of the ditch.

"What's wrong? Are you hurt?"

"No, but my legs won't work."

"You're just tired." He tucked his own revolver and holster where it belonged. "You'll be fine once we get you home to Verdeville." He crouched down, scooped me up like I was an open sack of expensive dog chow he didn't want to spill, and carried me to the tractor trailer. "Don't touch anything here. No prints from our team." Then he left and joined Eric.

Speechless again, I just stared after that strong, brave, capable man I'd known for a lifetime—those past five hours. Aunt Mary had surely mischaracterized Cousin Michael.

Beside me on the truck cab's outer step, Velma hugged me. "You okay?"

"Scared. Think I ruined your clothes."

"No problem, Tricia. I didn't like those jeans anyhow."

"How about you? That was pretty gutsy, what you did."

"Scared spitless," she said with a shudder. "Tonight was too close to the edge. I think my days of exhalationism are over."

It wouldn't do to correct her. "None of us are hurt?"

"Only the one you call Baldy, as far as I know, and he's just got a big knot on his head. Ought to look real cute with no hair on it."

Mike returned and patted my shoulder. "Feel better now?"

"Guess so. But what happens next?"

A sound like ripping cloth carried across the highway. In the dark, it was hard to be certain, but it looked as if Eric and Hippie were duct-taping Mr. Big's wrists behind his back. Also the other thug. Both were wounded, I had no clue how badly, but they'd receive medical attention when the sheriff's deputies found the rig in a few hours and opened up the trailer. They'd also find the nearby body of the driver, of course.

"Those three," said Mike, pointing to Skinny, Hippie, and Baldy, "will find a pay phone and notify the sheriff's substation, anonymously, of course."

The rumbling engine noise approaching from the west turned out to be Wrecker, bringing up his vehicle and backing it into position behind my poor car.

"Do we have to wait on the police?" I asked.

Mike grinned. "I'm leaving the sentry's license on the cab's step. It'll be pretty easy to locate him, the runners, their vehicles, and the missing bikes."

He made everything seem so simple—just another night at the office. "So they don't need us to testify or anything?"

"About what?" Mike said with a totally straight face. "We were never here."

15

On the quiet ride back to Marrowbone, I finally relaxed securely as Mike's strong arm held me tightly in the back seat. It bothered me how I felt about my twice-removed third cousin-in-law—namely, that I liked him a whole lot more and in vastly different ways than seemed appropriate. I felt close to him, but not a familial proximity. This was bigger, deeper, more intense—as best I could remember it, this felt like I was in love.

And, even with a distant cousin, that made me feel icky.

It was 1:55 a.m. when Wrecker unloaded my car in front of Eric's garage. He grabbed a beer, slapped Eric and Mike on their upper backs, and started walking away.

I tugged Wrecker's shirtsleeve to break his stride. "Thanks for bringing my car to safety. Sorry it was so much trouble."

The moonlight reflected off his dazzling white teeth. "No problem, Tricia."

"I, uh, don't have any cash on me, but I can send…"

"No charge." He held up the pale palm of his dark hand. "It's just a simple little favor I did for a buddy."

Unbelievable. Considering I'd been so prickly about picking up a relative from the bus stop… "But I can't let you go without thanking you properly."

"For a ten-mile tow," he said, grinning, "let's call it one hug."

I embraced him like I would've a favorite cousin I hadn't seen in months. He was such a large man, my arms didn't even fit all the way around him. "Thanks."

"I'd better get going before my wife calls the cops," he said, patting my shoulder as he disengaged. "And cops is one thing we don't really want right now, do we?"

"No, guess not."

As Wrecker drove his truck toward home, I realized I'd never even learned his real name.

Skinny phoned with a report that everyone had gotten back home safely after making their anonymous call. Then Mike and Eric took two beers to the garage out back and worked on my car—replacing a bad thermostat, I was told. Daisy-Dawg followed and monitored their work with both eyes closed.

I unloaded the snubby—three live cartridges and two empty cases—and placed everything, plus the holster, on the kitchen table.

Velma changed from her optic orange bikini to a fairly normal looking set of pajamas. I really wanted to soak in a hot bath with a margarita in each hand, but Eric's place had only a stall shower and cold beer.

Since she'd already tossed my original torn clothes into her washing machine, Velma found me another pair of jeans she didn't like and a clean t-shirt she could live without. Both fit better than her first set of loaners.

When I'd dried off and re-dressed, Velma sat me down. "It's okay for cousins to fall in love... especially if they're not on the *blood* side of the family."

"What?"

"At the worst it's just tacky, and then only if somebody makes a fuss."

Not going there. "I don't want to discuss..."

But Vema did. "You know... the goo-goo eyes, all the snuggling."

I shook my head. "I hardly know him. Never met him before tonight. Just picked him up as a favor..."

"Maybe you can fool yourself, Tricia, but you can't fool me. You fell hard for Mike." Then Velma smiled. "Not that I blame you. He's a hunk. Pretty cool under pressure, too."

"I can't."

"You *are*. Just face it like a woman and deal with it." She leaned so close I could smell the ham and cheese on her breath from hours before. "If you walk away from Mike because he's somewhere in your family's in-law tree, you'll regret it for the rest of your life." She studied my face for a reaction, then stretched. "I'm going to bed. Tell Eric not to wake me up either."

And she closed the bedroom door behind her, leaving me alone with several uncomfortable thoughts.

A full ten minutes later, the two mechanics came back inside, rubbing their greasy hands with shop towels. Mike held up a little gizmo that looked like a 1950s movie flying saucer. "Stuck thermostat. All fixed."

"My car's running again?"

"Good as new," added Eric, opening a fresh beer for

himself and tossing another to Mike.

When they went back to the front porch, I grabbed the blanket throw and joined them. Daisy-Dawg was waiting by Eric's customary rocker.

"What you gonna do with that badass bike out there?" asked Eric, after a hearty belch.

Mike grinned. "I was hoping you'd have a suggestion."

Eric scratched the dog's ear. "Well, if you was to leave it parked against that big oak tree down there by the pond and I was to find it tomorrow morning, I wouldn't have any way of knowing how it got there, would I?"

Mike thoughtfully rubbed some condensation from his beer can. "Guess not."

"And I wouldn't have any reason to suspect it was part of some big truck load that was hijacked, would I?"

"Good point." Mike raised his beer appreciatively.

"And unless that county's sheriff happened to be looking in Marrowbone for a Harley stolen in Hermitage, he wouldn't be traipsing around out here anyhow, would he?"

"Not unless he has a Catahoula Cur," said Mike.

Big grin. Then Eric turned toward me. "I like this fella, Tricia. Try not to toss this one back so quick."

My face heated up. "He's my third cousin-in-law twice removed… remember?"

"No blood," said Eric. "And y'all don't look anything alike, by the way."

Mike just sipped his brew and acted like he wasn't the primary topic of our conversation.

"Thanks for all your help tonight, Eric." I had to change the uncomfortable topic. "But I've really got to get home to Verdeville. I've got this big audit…"

Mike stood. "Yeah, we should go. Evidently I'm expected for some hunting junket."

"Nothing in season but varmints and maybe ducks."

"Whatever. I wasn't traveling to hunt anyhow."

That brought to mind an old, unsettled topic. "So why *were* you riding the bus to Nashville, Mike?"

"Just on my way to Knoxville, looking for places I've never been and doing things I've never done."

Eric eyed him soberly. "I'll wager you've done some, uh, *envelopments* before."

Just a nod.

"It is what it is." After a soft chuckle, Eric spoke to Daisy-Dawg as he patted her rump. "Let's go on inside and get to bed so these folks can go home." Then he gave me a sideways friend-hug and shook hands with Mike. As they'd done before, they gripped tighter than necessary and held it longer. The first time, I'd perceived it as them testing each other. This time it seemed more like non-verbal congratulations on a job well done. Of course, you'd have to understand man-communication to know for certain.

Mike and I rolled the Harley down behind that big oak and he carefully wiped down the handlebars and seat.

"I probably touched that back rest, too."

He silently cleaned it.

"If they're really determined, they might find a trace of my DNA on the rear seat. Things got a little dicey during our first getaway."

He nodded. "Maybe mine, too." Then he laughed and hugged me.

Standing by the pond, leaning next to the big oak at nearly 2:30 a.m., I suddenly felt more awake and alive than I could remember since my first year at college. I wrapped my arms around Mike and squeezed like I needed to become part of him.

He propped up my chin, looked deeply into my eyes, and kissed me.

At first, startled, I nearly pulled away. But after an instant, I melted and my brain forgot all about cousins and seconds and thirds and in-laws. Our kiss lasted for hours… or maybe less than a minute. Difficult to say. Then there were scant inches between our faces—barely far enough apart for him to be in focus.

"Eric's right, you know," he said, licking his lips as though he didn't want to miss any flavoring.

"About what?" Face now nestled into his upper chest, my voice was muffled. Heart raced and my legs tingled.

"We're not blood kin."

"Mike, I don't want to talk about that."

"We need to. I can't let you go. Not now." With the moonlight reflecting off the small pond, he searched my eyes again. "I can't walk around you at gatherings of the combined families and pretend we're just *whatever* cousins. We're a lot more."

"But what are we?"

"Not sure. But I know it's more."

"How could you know that, Mike?"

"The same way I knew exactly where you were on the highway slope and had a pretty good idea of what you were doing."

"Telepathy?"

"More than that. A connection… something intense."

I felt it, too, but couldn't admit it. Not to my twice-removed third cousin-in-law. Not if it meant something existed that I simply could not acknowledge.

16

I was too frazzled to operate the vehicle, so Mike drove. Finally leaving behind Marrowbone's single, non-functioning traffic light at about 2:40 a.m., we stayed on Highway 70 and rode silently for a few minutes before Mike surprised me with a question of sorts.

"You've mentioned this big audit several times. Sounds like it's got you all knotted up."

"It does. Besides which, Mr. Dross *keeps* my innards churning—shovels huge responsibility on me but apparently doesn't trust me to do it properly. Won't leave me alone and let me work." I scanned the black landscape hurtling past my Toyota. "These corporate auditors hit about ten per cent of their franchise offices each fall, before the federal tax season really cranks up. But this will be the first time they've stumbled into Verdeville since I've been working there."

He patted my knee with his large, warm hand. "Relax, Tricia. You're already prepared. You've done your work faithfully and thoroughly. The worst they can do is try to throw you off balance to see if you shake easily. You don't— you proved that tonight. So don't let those corporate suits rattle you, not one iota. You've got this."

His words warmed me. It was the best pep talk I'd had since Aunt Mary encouraged me prior to a panel discussion I'd had to chair in middle school speech class.

By the time I'd thanked Mike in a few halting words, we'd reached Verdeville's city limits, roughly ten minutes from Marrowbone. Being a rather sleepy town even during peak business hours, it scarcely exhibited a pulse during the dark hours of the morning.

The other reason I'd let Mike drive was because I'd needed more time to study him. Time not fraught with bullies assaulting young women or hijackers trying to kill us. I needed to figure out what to do about a twice-removed third cousin-in-law who'd recaptured my car and saved my butt, then kissed and embraced me like I'd never experienced before.

One thing, however, was finally settled—or at least fully rationalized. I'd decided to accept the studied verdicts of Judge Eric and Jurist Velma that there was no blood between Mike and me... and therefore no legal restraints on how close we could become. Of course, that said nothing about propriety and whether I'd have to endure the disapproving clucks of family members (on whichever side) if I *was* able to diminish our distance.

Not to mention I knew rather little concerning how Mike felt about me. Attracted to me? *Sure.* Willing to risk his life for me? *Uh... evidently.* But was he in town merely for a quick varmint-hunting trip, a race to Knoxville, and then return to wherever he'd been? One of many topics we'd never had a chance to broach. In fact, we'd discussed hardly anything besides the multiple crises we'd faced so far that long night.

What *was* the future for kin who weren't really kin... who kissed each other with that much heat? Whenever I'd heard of kissing cousins, I'd always imagined a shy peck on the cheek or maybe a crush like I'd had on Eric as a wide-eyed freshman. Certainly nothing like the intensity, the passion... the abandon I'd felt in Mike's embrace.

Watching him intently as he drove through downtown and turned north on Highway 141, I considered rehearsing a little speech. Something about how we had to forget every-thing we'd experienced in the preceding several hours and just move on with our separate lives. *Nah.* Maybe my soliloquy should propose continuing an illicit relationship which no one—absolutely no one—could ever learn about. *Nope.* What was left? The speech about coming clean with the family and letting them decide our fates? *Never.*

Before I could decide which text to rehearse, I pointed out the approaching turn from 141, east into the quiet, set-tled subdivision which included the home of Aunt Mary and Uncle Cleve. It was 2:55 a.m. As exhausted as I was, I would've much preferred to go straight to my own apart-ment, southeast of town, but my mission had been to deliver Cousin Michael to Auntie. I was a lot of things and had failed at many aspects of my life, but when I said I'd do someone a simple little favor, I'd do it or die trying. *Ha. Very nearly did die trying with tonight's little favor!*

Despite Mike's pep talk, I was still worried about Mon-day morning's big audit and coping with my supervisor's interfering panic, but both paled compared to my fear that I might in a few moments be saying farewell to a man who'd become an important part of me. Not sure which part, of course.

Auntie's was the last house on the left, before the properties curled into the wedges of their cul-de-sac. Fearing the lump in my throat would prevent speech, I just pointed and Mike turned into the driveway. Inside, lights were on—a living room lamp and the kitchen overhead—so somebody was presumably still awake and waiting for us.

Still in the car, my right hand on the door handle, I applied pressure, but not quite enough to trip the latch. Mike clutched my left wrist and said, "Wait."

"For what?" It was already 3 a.m. "We can't linger in the driveway this late without neighbors talking."

"Let them talk." He held my hand tenderly. "We need some time."

I gulped. One eye on Auntie's front door, I tried with the other to discern why Mike wanted time. "For what?"

"Us. We're not as prohibitively close as you seem to think. I mean, like your friends said, no blood between us at all." He let that register. "Besides, I, uh, I think we'd be good together."

"Together as what?" Hoped he wouldn't say conjoined cousins.

"*Together* together." He held up my hand and kissed my fingertips. "Tricia, I have a sixth sense." He looked over his shoulder as he said it. "You've seen it, you know it's real. I can sense things which can't be explained. And this sense tells me we belong together."

"But as what?"

"Well, eventually… lovers." The warmth of that noun evidently embarrassed him as much as it did me.

I stared at my fingertips, still moist from his lips. "Even

with the cousin stuff aside, a series of crises like we've had tonight is not the basis for starting a great relationship."

Mike closed his eyes for a moment. "Actually, throughout literature, that's exactly how great relationships take root."

"Exactly which literature?" I was picturing disaster movies.

"Well, for starters, you see it a lot in comic books and graphic novels."

"Oh, the classics."

His smile revealed how serious he wasn't. "Can't think of any in particular, but I know a good librarian back home."

Where is home? But I was silent.

"What will it take to convince you, Tricia?"

"I'd need a lot more than your sixth or seventh sense. And just because Eric and Velma gave us a green light to, um, get together, it doesn't mean anybody else would accept our decision." I'd seen films where men were bullwhipped and women sent off to nunneries. Earlier times, of course.

He squeezed my hand but seemed unaware he was doing so.

"We ought to go inside, Mike. They're waiting." I pointed to the lighted house.

"I can tell you're confused. Heck, I'm a little surprised myself. Never expected to find you when I set out Sunday morning from Lansing."

"Lansing?" So it *was* an "M" state. "I thought you came from somewhere in Missouri."

"Uh, nope. Never been there."

"But Auntie said... Oh, never mind. My brain's too flummoxed." Once more, I reached for the door handle, but Mike stopped me again.

"Okay, things have settled down and we're no longer in danger. Now, which part confuses you the most?"

17

No sense letting him resume explaining things to me. My dashboard clock indicated 3:10 a.m. and I yawned with no restraint. "It's been a really long night. I don't see any movement inside, so better let me go first." I patted his right knee lightly. "You okay to wait out here for another minute?"

Clearly disappointed, he merely nodded.

When I exited and walked up the driveway, I realized how stiff and sore I was, in addition to battered and completely exhausted. The front door was unlocked, so I just opened it and stepped into the living space, where one lamp burned near the end of the couch.

Aunt Mary had been dozing in her easy chair but bolted upright when I entered. She threw off a blanket, rushed over, and hugged me tightly. "Where have you been? We've been worried sick. What has happened to your clothes? I've called your phone 96 times."

"I borrowed these clothes, but I'll have to explain later." She alternately hugged and chastised me as she steered me into the kitchen, where the brighter light revealed how haggard I was. If I looked as awful as I felt, she'd probably call for an ambulance.

"What on earth happened to you, dear?" Panic filled her eyes.

"It's a long story, Aunt Mary, but there's not enough time now. I have a big meeting in a few hours and I've got to crash." I reached for the back of a kitchen chair to steady myself. "But I came through for you. My errand's complete... I've brought your cousin Michael."

Her gentle hands stroked my upper arms softly. "What do you mean, dear?"

"You asked me to pick him up, so I did. We would've been here hours ago, but there were some, uh, problems on the road."

"Picked up *who*?"

"Cousin Michael."

Auntie squinted into my eyes. "Cousin Michael's here in bed, dear. They're already packed for their hunting trip and plan to set out around dawn."

Something inside me froze solid. "Can't be. I've been with him since around nine o'clock."

She clutched my shoulders and shoved me into the same chair I'd been using to prop myself up. "Been with who?"

"Your cousin Michael, from the bus stop."

"No, dear. When Michael's bus arrived a few minutes early and nobody was there to meet him, he called the house. We figured you'd been held up in traffic and I assumed I could reach you to let you know we didn't need that little favor any more."

Probably the most impactful call I've ever missed. My heart started hammering again.

"I told your Uncle Cleve to phone his friend that works at a Nashville hospital. He's in maintenance and I knew he got off around eight. So it was Cleve's friend who zipped over to the bus station to pick up Cousin Michael."

Why didn't the friend get suckered into this favor in the first place? I couldn't keep the tartness out of my voice. "Wish I'd known about that."

"Like I said, dear, I tried to call you but never got through."

"Well, Uncle Cleve didn't clue me in either, after I reached him on a borrowed phone. My battery's dead."

"Sometimes Cleve doesn't hear so well on the phone," said Auntie, "which is why he hardly ever uses it. Of course, if he'd get a hearing aid like I've been trying..."

Ugh. I had to blot out the rest of her tiresome topic. My uncle would never get a hearing aid and I'd probably always be the victim on the other end of his doomed phone calls. "Well, since I thought the cousin still needed a ride, I was just trying to confirm with Uncle Cleve which bus Michael was on and when it was due in Nashville." Wasn't getting anywhere. "We were both at the same depot, probably only a few minutes apart. Can't believe I totally missed him."

"Not by much. He's right here in bed," she repeated as she pointed toward the short hallway.

My eyes bulged. "Are you positive it's Michael?"

"I suppose I'd know my own Lennitt cousin, dear, no matter how distant."

So that's her maiden name. I peered around the corner

toward the nearest of the two small guest bedrooms and heard raw snoring, but couldn't see anything. "If that person's our distant cousin, who's the guy out in my car?"

"Bring him inside and we'll have a look."

I slumped over so exhaustedly that my head whacked the table. "Impossible."

Auntie scurried to her front door, presumably intending to trot outside to my car, but Mike was already leaning on the door when she opened it.

"Aunt Mary?" he asked, extending his hand.

She staggered backward, obviously startled at *his* haggard appearance. "Well, y-yes, I suppose s-so. C-come on in, I guess."

I couldn't bear to watch any longer and closed my eyes. But their conversation reached me anyway.

"You probably don't recognize me. And, like I told Tricia, I don't know a lot about the extended family that moved away from the Lansing area."

"Lansing, Michigan? Why, I've never even been anywhere near Lansing."

"Guess that explains why we've never met. Unless it was when I was too little to remember. Maybe at that lake in your photo."

"Photo? Lake? Who did you say you were?"

"Cousin Michael. Mike Stagg."

Since my ears were already following, I couldn't bear *not* to watch, so I opened my eyes.

Auntie looked profoundly puzzled. "Well, what are you doing here in Verdeville?"

"I've been asking myself that same thing over the past several hours. I'd never heard of this place 'til Tricia caught up with me at the bus station and explained where we were heading."

The wrong Michael. I would never hear the end of this. Closed my eyes again.

"Where on earth did you intend to go?"

"Like I told Tricia, to Knoxville and then nowhere in particular. I thought it was pretty cool to bump into a relative and have an offer of a room." He looked into the kitchen and spotted my dead body, too exhausted and shocked to move. "Uh, assuming that offer's still open, I mean." Then he whispered and pointed. "Is she okay?"

"You tell me, Michael Stagg. You're no kin to me. What the blazes have you been doing to my niece this whole long night? And where are her clothes?"

At that point, I struggled from the kitchen table and staggered to the entryway of the living space. "Aunt Mary, Mike has not been molesting me. We're both a little, uh, tousled because we ran into some trouble."

"I'll want to hear all about that trouble, but first things first." She waggled an arthritic finger in my direction. "Young lady, picking up strangers is uncautious, but I'll deal with you later."

All I could do was shrug and even that minimal effort displayed my total exhaustion. Spotting a cell phone plugged in near the toaster, I asked whose it was.

"That's your cousin Michael's phone, dear. Why?"

I examined it. Fully charged. "Looks like the same kind of charger mine uses. Okay if I borrow it?"

"As long as Michael has it back by dawn, I suppose so."

I unhooked his phone and placed it next to the sunglasses I was certain were not Uncle Cleve's. Then I rummaged through my purse and plugged in my own phone. After I closed my eyes for a few hours, I'd need to check for new frantic messages from Mr. Dross. "Anybody mind if I crash?"

"You go ahead, dear. Right now, this young man and I will have a nice long talk."

As I passed Mike in the kitchen's entryway I gripped his elbow in solidarity, but his eyes were on Auntie.

"So you're *not* my Aunt Mary?" He was slow on the uptake. Mike seemed more worried about this confab than he had during most of the conflicts we'd already faced that night.

I guess nearly everybody's got an Aunt Mary somewhere on their family tree. For that matter, nearly every family likely has a Mike or Michael. It was almost 3:30 a.m. and I was too wearied to argue for either party, plus had no means to protect him from Auntie's possible wrath anyhow. Without sufficient time or energy to drive home in the few hours which remained, I had to close my eyes or I'd keel over. So I crawled onto the couch, curled up under Auntie's blanket, and hoped I could catch a few minutes of sleep.

"I'm Mary Lennitt Nolan," she told him brusquely. "Have you any aunts with that name?"

"No, ma'am. I expect not." Mike dutifully followed Aunt Mary into the kitchen, and I swear I saw him shudder as Auntie sat him down at the table like a weakened prisoner. She began by sermonizing about a gentleman's responsibilities regarding the proper treatment of innocent young ladies. I made a mental note—later, after proper rest—to gently update Auntie that there was little left of my *innocence*, though only a fraction of that particular education had come at the hands of Mike Stagg. So far.

I wasn't actually worried about Mike holding his own, however. In the past few hours, he'd whipped two armed criminals and a woman-beating bully in hand-to-hand combat—surely he could handle an unarmed woman in her seventies. I knew his charm and ease would quickly resurface and surely win over Aunt Mary. She was, after all, a human female.

And I was right, because he hurriedly regained high ground and his smooth confidence played her like a mellow cello.

Before fatigue overwhelmed me, their last conversational fragment I heard was Mike saying, "Everything's okay, we're no longer in danger, and I've brought your niece home safely, Mizz Nolan. Now, which part confuses you the most?"

18

After a nightmare ripped straight from our encounter with the hijackers, I woke disoriented to find myself in Auntie's second guest bedroom. It was 7:30 a.m., so I'd gotten roughly four hours sleep. Not nearly sufficient, considering all I'd been through, but hopefully enough to cope with the drama of Mr. Dross and our morning meeting with the corporate auditors.

Aunt Mary had been listening for me to waken and hustled in. "I sent Cleve over to your apartment to get you some fresh clothes. Nobody's in the bathroom right this minute, so you have time for a quick shower at least." Somehow realizing I could barely cope, Auntie was organizing me. "After you get out of the shower, we'll try to cover up the most visible cuts, scrapes, and abrasions." Presumably she meant makeup, though some areas might require plaster of Paris. "Your coffee's waiting after you dry off."

"Where's Michael?"

"Which one?" Her expression belied the question. She knew.

"The one I hauled all over middle Tennessee last night."

"He's in the other guest room."

"Mike's bunking with Michael?"

"No, dear, *my* Michael left at dawn with your Uncle Cleve, right after he came back with your clothes." She pointed to a pile of slacks and tops next to a pair of heels I never wore. "Cleve is still color blind so I just told him to grab a few of each. Maybe we can match something."

Doubtful. I just groaned.

"I told him to go with slacks since your legs are so cut up."

"Thanks." I clutched her arm before she could dash away. "How did I get in here?"

"Michael carried you." A crooked smile. "And don't ask which Michael."

I already knew. Thought I'd dreamed that lovely scene… long before the nightmare began.

"Now, go hurry with your shower so we can have a minute to talk before you leave for work. Get in the bathroom before your Michael wakes up and hogs it."

I couldn't even guess at the content of their conversation after I'd fallen into a coma, but gathered from Auntie's chipper tone that they'd settled things to her satisfaction. Mike had a way of explaining the most bizarre circumstances and making them sound halfway normal.

I nearly dozed in the shower, but my brain was pounding simultaneously on two different doors: one, gear up for Mr. Dross and the 9 a.m. audit shakedown. Two, rehearse a speech for Mike. I had the first one reasonably covered since all the budget material and supporting documentation was scrupulously organized in my desk. But the second matter was still an enigma wrapped in a conundrum, draped with chaos—to paraphrase some world leader of the distant past... or an NFL coach of last week's post-game press conference.

Maybe Auntie's coffee would help me decide which speech to deliver, if I had a few minutes of overlap with Mike before I had to fly to work. *Hmm... overlap with Mike.* I dried off, selected the slacks and blouse least offensively matched, and trudged into the kitchen holding the peekaboo heels Uncle Cleve had located in an unused corner of my closet. Auntie was just then pouring my coffee.

She watched silently as I remembered my phone, saw that it had charged sufficiently before Michael Lennitt had reclaimed his cord at dawn, and quickly checked my messages. Auntie had exaggerated with her claim of 96 calls. But she *had* called seventeen times, at approximate twenty minute intervals from 9 p.m. to 2:40 a.m. She likely would've phoned again at 3:00 a.m. but she'd finally dozed off and we were already inside Verdeville by that point anyhow.

And there were five short, urgent voice mails from Mr. Dross on Sunday—between about 9 p.m. when my phone had died and 10 p.m. when even he'd figured it was too late to phone about business. The first was a reminder to do what I'd already done, namely have all the material organized and complete. Each subsequent message was a different reminder of some other aspect of my job which I routinely performed. I laid my phone on the counter, took a sip of coffee, and squeezed my eyes shut.

I replayed the fifth and final message, which featured his strained voice, anxious and impatient that I had not returned any of his Sunday night calls—when I was *supposed* to be on vacation through Monday. Had to put down the phone again and grip the kitchen counter before I screamed. My job as his office manager was not overly difficult in itself, but Dross complicated everything by his contradictory practice of doing almost no visible work of his own, abutted to his pathological need to watch nearly all *my* work being done. And in times of crisis, like this surprise audit, Dross had the bizarre compulsion to touch nearly every item as though each needed his blessing to be properly dispatched.

Dross would be the death of me this morning. *Unless.* I suddenly flashed back to that frozen instant when Mr. Big, with a loaded gun in my face, lunged toward me in the highway ditch. And I shot him. Didn't do much damage, it turned out, but I was *willing* to put him down to save my own skin.

No, I don't mean I should shoot my boss. But I did realize I'd shown a lot more moxie out on that dark highway than I'd ever manifested in the office with Mr. Dross. And maybe, just maybe, I should be a bit more assertive at work... if I wanted to keep any shred of sanity. Another sip of caffeine to steel my nerves. Then, to his fifth voice message, I rehearsed and recorded this reply:

"Mr. Dross, it's Tricia Pilgrim. I was out of town for my floating holiday, as you already know. My phone died and my charger was misplaced. I've just now heard your messages and I'll be in the office by 8:50 this morning. All the pertinent material is ready for these inspectors. My spreadsheets and reports are pretty much always current except for the most recent day's activity or an incomplete time cycle. There's no need for you to be anxious and I don't require any additional reminders to handle my work assignments. Everything's covered, but if we confront any surprises, we'll adapt. I'll be there in plenty of time to discuss whatever still

confuses you the most."

I put down my phone. Either I'd just generated my own pink slip or I would begin a new chapter at work with Mr. Dross. Either way, I felt a lot better as I plopped down on the nearest kitchen chair.

Aunt Mary had merely watched my performance with wide eyes. It was easy to comprehend why she kept her simple, non-voicemail wall phone. "I told you I'd called 96 times."

No point in correcting her tally.

She eyed me closely. "We may have straightened out the two Michaels, dear, but I think you're a different Tricia than the one who left Verdeville Friday evening."

I nodded. Mike had willingly helped Shondell and brought the hijackers to justice. Eric and friends had cheerfully dropped everything to help us get my car back. And most of that time I'd been thinking only of myself and my audit. But that attitude and behavior was going to change.

Auntie was right, I was different, but hearing someone else say it brought tears to my eyes.

"What's wrong, dear?"

"Nothing." I dabbed my eyes. "I'm sorry we took so long, Aunt Mary, but we had a few detours."

"So I understand. How is Eric Prima these days?"

It appeared she had received a thorough briefing about our fateful night, but maybe Mike hadn't mentioned Velma's optic orange bikini. Some things it would be uncautious to tell my aunt about. "Eric's okay. As wild as ever." I took too large of a sip and the coffee burned all the way down. Also realized how hungry I was.

"I suppose you already know," said Aunt Mary as she handed me a dessert plate with two slices of warm toast, "your Michael was an MP in the Army."

"No, I didn't. That's more information than I've gotten from him."

"Well, dear, maybe you weren't asking the right questions." She slid over the jelly jar and a spoon.

"Didn't have a lot of time for interrogation. And when we did have a lull, it was difficult to squeeze any info out of him."

"Maybe you weren't squeezing the right places." She gave me a funny look. "Never mind. If your new friend is willing to stay around, your uncle has a contact in the Verdeville PD who'd be willing to give him an interview."

He'd mentioned something about settling down, but I'd assumed he'd been just thinking out loud. "I doubt he's sticking around here. Mike's a drifter." I took a bite of toast. "I've seen his type in movies… just bounces from one happenstance to another, from one woman…"

"Or maybe not, dear. Cleve's already spoken to him about the police department vacancy."

"They've met?"

"When Cleve and Cousin Michael were stumbling around this morning, your Michael woke up and chatted for a bit. He seemed very pleased."

"You're kidding."

"Ask him when he gets up."

I would. "But you know, there could be fifty guys applying for that job."

"Hardly any applicants, typically, according to Cleve. Unless your Michael exaggerated his experience or messes up the interview, I'd wager he's a shoo-in. The chief of police knows your uncle's a wonderful judge of character. If my husband vouches for somebody, you can take him to the bank."

"Well, I've already driven him everywhere else, so we may as well include the bank."

My aunt watched as I hurriedly finished the toast and drained the coffee cup. "You do realize, dear, it was uncautious of you to pick up a total stranger."

Ugh... I'll never live this down. "I thought he was Cousin Michael."

My aunt eyed me levelly without blinking. "No, dear. He looks nothing at all like my cousin."

As if I could've known.

At that moment, a bare-chested Mike entered the kitchen in his borrowed PJ bottoms, which were too loose and drooping on his hips.

Blushing furiously, Aunt Mary left the kitchen—to give us some privacy, I assumed—but returned in a moment with one of her husband's t-shirts. "It's uncautious to see a man's nipples before breakfast."

"Sorry, Mizz Nolan." And he hurriedly shrugged into the shirt. Only his shoulders filled it out; the rest was for a shorter man with considerable belly. Then he turned to me. "Do we have a few minutes before you go?"

Eyeing the kitchen clock, 8 a.m., I calculated. "Thirty-four minutes, minus the time it takes to brush my teeth, before I have to fly out the door."

"Well," Mike said, after grabbing a mug and plopping into the chair next to mine, "this shouldn't take too long."

I flinched. The last time I'd heard those words was in college when the bratty frat guy told me he'd found someone "better" for him.

19

I was about to be dumped again. Cold certain. Just as I'd decided to adopt a fresh outlook about helping others, being kinder and more giving… it jerked up and bit me.

Mike slurped his coffee and scrutinized my face. "Well, we had quite a time last night, didn't we?"

I nodded soberly.

"I'm, uh, sorry…"

Here it comes.

"…that I turned out to be the wrong Michael."

Wait. Rewind the tape. That didn't sound like dumping language. "Huh?"

"You know, me being at the bus station at about the same time as your cousin and all." His stomach rumbled. "And how much trouble it caused you, since you thought I was him. And me just going with the flow because it seemed plausible we might be distant kin. In this case, of course, me being the wrong Mike."

He must be nervous because he's rambling. I'd not seen him anxious before that moment, except when it seemed Auntie would read him the riot act. "Not the wrong one *per se.* Just a different Mike from who I was expecting."

More abdominal noises. "Different last name, totally distinct family, even coming from another state..."

"Easy mistake. Could've happened to anybody." I got up, grabbed the bread, and dropped two slices in Auntie's super-efficient toaster.

"But, in spite of nothing being in sync, everything still seemed to fit."

My arched eyebrows conveyed my puzzlement.

"I mean between us. You know, uh, more than cousins."

"I still don't see how we could spend that much time together and never work out that the fundamental facts didn't match whatsoever." The toast popped up sooner than expected and startled me. "I've spent several recent years carefully weighing and analyzing everything..."

"Some folks need lots of structure and predictability."

"...and the first impulsive thing I did since college was dash off to Memphis to chill with a few girlfriends." Still standing, I began spreading jelly on the toast before I realized it was Mike's. *Maybe he's a butter guy.* "That turned out to be a fiasco and I was miserable. All I wanted was to limp straight home and lick my wounds... and I vowed never again to veer off my schedule or my map."

"Which we never even caught sight of last night." He gobbled half a piece of toast and chewed vigorously.

"Nope." I clutched the back of my chair. "All that went out the window when Auntie called with just one simple favor."

Another huge bite. "Pick up Cousin Michael."

I eyed the clock—8:05 a.m. Mr. Dross would be a drooling lunatic if I didn't arrive well before nine. Back to Mike. "And I ended up with you instead." I wanted to sit again, but we needed to wrap this up.

Mike swallowed hurriedly. "Disappointed?"

In any romance novel, this was the juncture when my answer would have to be absolutely perfect—it had to convey how much I'd fallen for him, how relieved I was that we *weren't* cousins, and how worried I was that he might not be commensurately crazy about me. But I hadn't had time to prepare a response and any meaningful words stalled in my throat. So I did the next best thing—picked up a napkin and dabbed some toast crumbs from his inviting lips.

His large tanned hand covered mine and he slowly moved the napkin—my hand still attached—over his complete mouth. Then he dropped the napkin to the table and lightly kissed my fingertips. Again with the fingertips. I shuddered deliciously.

Sometimes, I guess, you don't need prepared text. I didn't understand how fingertips and lips could be so erotic, but wasn't about to complain.

Monitoring my eyes carefully, he released my hand and took a sip of coffee.

"Are you one of those guys who just drifts around? You know, spend nine years in college and seven years in grad school?"

"No. I spent nine *semesters* in college. Then enlisted in the Army. I've considered grad school, but think I'd rather settle down somewhere."

"What about your job back home?"

"I'm between jobs."

I'd need to learn more about that later. "Where do you want to settle?"

"I'm pretty much content wherever I am." He gazed out the window into the bright morning light. "This town of Verdeville, at least the little bit I've seen so far, seems to have everything I want."

"What *do* you want, Mike?" I had to sit back down for this. And clutched my cup so my hands wouldn't visibly shake.

"Kind folks, a sweet spirit of community." He gulped. "A compatible woman to share my life with."

My reaction spilled some coffee. His word *compatible* worried me... mostly because we seemed complete opposites. "Are you always this direct?"

"My parents used to say I was overly earnest at times and teased me about changing my name to Ernest. But how can a person be too earnest?"

Not a clue. My hands slightly trembled as I tamped a napkin over the spill.

"Tricia, I know you're tired and you have to hustle away to work, but I thought you should know my intentions."

"Which are?"

"To settle here, find a job, see if a woman I met is as interested in me as I am in her."

My heart thudded like it had when I'd jumped off the high diving platform at age seven. "But I scarcely know you, Mike."

"Not true. We've been together, non-stop except for our short morning naps, for the past eleven hours at least. You know all about me."

"Not where you've been... or where you're going."

"But I'm not going... I'm staying," Mike said softly. "And you'll find out where I've been as you get to know me better."

"Judging from the way you fight, you've evidently visited some hard places."

"I only fight when it's important and when reason won't turn the tables. And besides, you handled yourself pretty well, also."

"I was totally scared almost the whole night."

"Me, too, at times," said Mike, as his long thick fingers fidgeted with his napkin.

"You never looked frightened."

"Glad of it. We needed every trump we could find."

My brain strained for snippets of a speech I felt I was supposed to deliver. "Remember, they say relationships born out of crisis situations can never last."

"Possibly so, Tricia. But they also say coffee's poison and bacon will kill you."

"In other words, life is too short..." I checked the time again. "Look, I've got this awful meeting in a few minutes. But after that I can chill a little... and hopefully think better."

"And if I can borrow a car, I need to drive my, uh, package, over to Knoxville."

I'd forgotten all about the marijuana for his dying friend. "I wish I could go with you, you know, to meet your lieutenant and thank him." My eyes filled. "Take as much time as you need."

"I will." He took one final sip of coffee, leaving a fulsome drop on his lips. "And you'll hold off on any big decisions 'til I get back? About us, I mean."

Pushing back my chair, I rose slowly, my mind checking neuro-data files for how to reply. *No, I must not overthink it*—because that was usually my downfall. Clearing my throat, I said, "I'll wait for you."

During his wide grin, his tongue found that errant drop of coffee on his lips. "So you agree it's worth a few days of non-pressure time together to see if we're as compatible as my sixth sense tells me we are?" The ever-confident Mike apparently needed some reassurance.

His need for validation made *me* feel more confident somehow. "Sometimes it takes me a full week of concentrated study before I can make up my mind about big stuff." I pretended I could hold back my own smile.

He stood and stretched all three hundred muscles in his upper body. "Let's make it two weeks. My research is detailed, in-depth, and generally lasts for hours at a time."

Mike tightly hugged me and gently kissed me, leaving the faint taste of caffeine and grape jelly on my mouth. I licked my lips, kissed him back... and then smiled. "After you get back, where do we begin?"

"We've already started the beginning." Another soft kiss. "And the end of the beginning might be some of the best parts."

"You'll have to show me all those parts when you get back from Knoxville."

My ex-cousin Mike hugged me so tightly I could scarcely breathe, then we kissed again. The same as our kiss by the pond, it lasted either an hour or a minute. Then he gazed into my eyes with his sixth or seventh sense. "Which part, Tricia, confuses you the most?"

Author's Acknowledgements

This is my third venture with the talented Gunnar Grey at her emerging press, *Dingbat Publishing*. Even though I produce good and entertaining stories, with each project I realize how much more there is to learn about writing and editing. I thank Mrs. Grey for her friendship, support, encouragement, expertise, and patience. And, of course, for extending a contract for this novella.

She also designed our cool cover!

I especially appreciate my stalwart beta reader—my own brother and fellow author, Charles A. Salter—who promptly read this manuscript and provided valuable feedback (as usual). And to my wife, Denise Williams Salter, who read a draft, helped me flesh out certain characters, and also provided many other helpful observations.

Thanks to my friend Theresa Thevenote for helping me establish how "Cousin Michael" could be related to Tricia through the marriage of her Aunt Mary (without Tricia knowing Michael's last name).

My brief fictional account of the character Lieutenant Ralph Tyler was inspired by a much more complex real life incident of my wife's uncle, Thomas A. Williams, while he was assigned to Strother Field near Winfield, Kansas during World War Two. During a training "dogfight," Lieutenant Williams discovered his P-47 engine was on fire. As recalled by his younger brother Paul Williams [around mid-2009] Thomas had two immediate, contradictory instincts: bail out, and attempt to redirect the plane's impact away from the houses and population below. He took care of the latter, but when he then attempted to bail out, he was restrained by his oxygen mask hose (or strap), which had gotten fouled. Thomas had to cut himself loose before he could separate from the aircraft. He was burned pretty badly (mostly on his arms, but also on his face).

Then, during descent, Thomas had difficulty grabbing his rip cord. [Evidently, while struggling to free himself, he must have cut (or torn) a strap holding the rip cord.] Free-falling at an incredible rate, he tried to grab the handle, but it kept whipping away. Eventually, he reeled in the strap hand over hand and finally was able to yank the handle and deploy the chute. He must have been pretty close to the ground by that time. He nearly landed in a river... until he yanked on his shroud lines and re-directed sufficiently.

Paul said the ambulance team raced to the site of the plane's crash—an empty field—to look for Thomas. Standard operating procedure was for the pilot—if able—to head back toward the crash, so Lieutenant Williams walked his way over to them. Somebody spotted him and everybody looked up. When he got within shouting range, he called out, "You guys looking for me?"

Thomas Williams had redirected his burning P-47 fighter so nobody was harmed by its crash, and he survived the complicated bail-out. Over six decades later, he died (in his eighties) after several years of intense pain and other serious medical problems.

About the Author

Romantic comedy and romantic suspense are among eleven completed novel manuscripts and four completed novellas. Several more on the way!

I'm co-author of two nonfiction monographs (about librarianship) with a royalty publisher, plus a signed chapter in another book and a signed article in a specialty encyclopedia. I've also published articles, book reviews, and over 120 poems; my writing has won nearly 40 awards, including several in national contests. As a newspaper photojournalist, I published about 150 bylined newspaper articles, and some 100 bylined photos.

I worked nearly 30 years in the field of librarianship. I'm a decorated veteran of U.S. Air Force (including a remote tour of duty in the Arctic, at Thule AB in N.W. Greenland).

I'm the married parent of two and grandparent of six.

Also by J.L. Salter

From Dingbat Publishing
Scratching the Seven-Month Itch
Curing the Uncommon Man-Cold
Amanda Moore or Less (two-book boxed set)
Duchess of Earl—coming soon!

From Clean Reads [Astraea Press]
The Overnighter's Secret
Rescued by that New Guy in Town
Called to Arms Again
Echo Taps
Don't Bet On It
Hid Wounded Reb
The Ghostess and MISTER Muir
Love and Diamonds (anthology)

From TouchPoint Press
Stuck on Cloud Eight—coming soon!

Another great read from Dingbat Publishing

AMANDA MOORE OR LESS

If Jason does have
the itch, Amanda is
after the tramp
who's scratching it.

Scratching
the
Seven-Month
Itch

J.L. SALTER   δ

a screwball romantic comedy

1

Friday, May 22, 2009

Amanda Moore knew from the *Maneater* ringtone which friend was calling: the older, bossy, impetuous one. "Hello?"

"Not sure how to tell you this, but... he's cheating." It came out so easily that Christine Powers must have practiced. A rather startling announcement, considering she didn't even say hello.

"Okay, *who's* cheating?"

Christine's tense silence provided the answer.

"Jason? No way!"

"I wouldn't have said anything, but the evidence is overwhelming."

"That's insane! Jason?" Amanda's voice quavered. "Who the heck with?"

"Not certain... yet."

"Exactly how reliable is this evidence if you don't even know who she is?"

"Overwhelming." Christine always sounded certain.

"Well, spit it out! And quick. My *perfect* sister Kaye will be here any minute!"

"Oh. Maybe we should wait 'til you're not in such a rush."

"Yeah, well, thanks a bunch for getting me all riled up when I don't have time to talk." Amanda scanned her duplex as she struggled to process two domestic emergencies on top of a new crisis at work. "Look, I know Jason's not playing around. But this is very important—Kaye canNOT know ANYthing about this!"

"Mum's the word." Christine probably thought Mum was a deodorant. "Call me later and I'll give you the rest of my intel. Bye."

Amanda flicked her phone shut without reply. Her honey brown hair framed an attractive face which barely avoided being beautiful. Her bright blue eyes could make someone melt or cause them a chill, depending on the person and circumstances. Right now they were icy. Christine, Kaye… and Jason were all ganging up on her.

She checked the kitchen clock—about two minutes until Hurricane Kaye's arrival. Though distinctly skeptical of this sudden accusation, Amanda worried anyway. She knew Jason Stewart better than she'd known any other man, but significant gaps remained. In fact, maybe they didn't really know each other all that well. After getting comfortable within their relationship, Amanda had stopped trying so hard to "learn" him. And probably vice versa.

But even if Jason were taking her for granted, it didn't mean he was playing around. "Jason wouldn't cheat on me. Why would he?" *But if he IS boffing someone else, he's a dead man.* Amanda examined her short, unpainted fingernails. *Might need something else to claw that slut's eyeballs… whoever she is.*

Outside the apartment, a car door slammed—her elder sister was literally seconds away. Amanda sucked in a quick breath. *Remember, keep a hard shell so Kaye won't find any weak spot to probe. And not a word about this Jason mess, because she will immediately tell Mom and Dad that I've lost another one.*

Amanda glanced down at her work heels and smoothed her skirt. Her only ace in the sibling race—she had even prettier legs than perfect Kaye.

The doorbell rang. *She's ba-aacckk!*

Amanda's hand trembled slightly when she turned the knob. "Hi, Kaye!" There wasn't time to invite her inside because Kaye Moore-Smith was already lunging forward. They hugged awkwardly, with noticeable space between them. *No bags?* "I didn't have time to move much since you called yesterday, but there's still room to sleep and that single bed is pretty comfortable." Amanda pointed down the short hallway. It had been about two years since she'd seen Kaye and they didn't talk much on the phone, either. "Come have a look."

When Kaye had toured shortly after Amanda moved in, she'd acted like nobody could survive in less than 2,000 square feet. Now Kaye assessed everything as though she wore white gloves. With higher grades, fuller bosom, better hair (dyed blonde, of course), Kaye had always seemed the favorite daughter. Growing up, she'd been bossy and rather cold... and eight years older. She'd married right after college, moved to an upscale Indianapolis neighborhood, and quickly produced a child... a big plus. With her looks and ability to role play, Kaye could sell anything; currently she represented high-end office equipment. But their parents ignored the facts: Kaye was separated with a pending divorce and her thirteen-year-old daughter was a witchy brat.

And Kaye was finally developing a belly! Amanda hid her glee.

When Kaye peeked into the cluttered guestroom, which Amanda used as an ad hoc storage depot, she wrinkled her nose and delivered a short speech (which sounded rehearsed) about needing space to spread out, so she would find suitable lodgings in Nashville, about 25 miles west. She'd be in the area for most of four days, Kaye had said, so perhaps her company was covering the hotel costs.

"You hear anything much from Mom and Dad?" In their predictable e-mail-and-Facebook sibling conversations, this was Kaye's opening move.

Amanda sighed. "Mom forwards nearly every e-mail she gets, especially the ones telling you to send it to ten people in the next minute so you'll have good luck."

Kaye nodded without replying. Evidently she received the same.

"But she rarely sends anything about herself."

"And Dad?" Kaye asked.

"He still won't use a computer." Amanda smiled, rather tentatively.

"Well, he doesn't use phones much either, as I recall. Unless Mom slaps it to his ear."

They laughed together—the first time in many years. Amanda thawed a bit. Perhaps this visit would be different; maybe they could be more than estranged sisters. Probably not friends, but it would be nice to share something more than coolish civility.

Funny, how Kaye always seemed to be looking for something better. *Must have been tough on her soon-to-be-ex-husband.*

"So, how are things with your, uh… legal proceedings?" Amanda didn't know if her sister wanted to discuss this.

"The divorce? Oh, it's dragging out, but the lawyers prefer it that way. Tom and I had mostly agreed on all the big issues, but they keep finding wrinkles that supposedly have to be documented up the ying-yang." Kaye frowned. "More fees for them, of course." Without warning, she blurted out, "He cheated on me." Then she clamped her lips shut and looked away.

Amanda felt her jaw dropping. That was the first divorce detail Kaye had volunteered. "Oh, Kaye, I'm sorry…" "Son of a gun was diddling somebody at work." Kaye's eyes reddened. "You want to know how I found out?"

Amanda *did* want to know… intensely. But—unlike celebrity breakups—with her perfect sister being the topic, it felt like prying. "No, you don't have to…"

"She left her nasty panties in Tom's glove compartment!"

They'd used his expensive BMW? *Shocking.* Her sibling was on the verge of tears and normally such pain would give Amanda a tiny bit of pleasure. But she just felt compassion, possibly for the first time since she'd been ten and Kaye had finally left for college eighteen years ago. "Your daughter… how's she adjusting?"

Kaye held her hand vertically. *Don't go there.* She and her witchy daughter had been at odds since Chelsea was nine, almost four years ago. Obviously the trip to Nashville was also an excuse for a beleaguered mom to just get away. Kaye shook her head. "I should leave. My reservation…"

Since she'd never intended to stay, why hadn't Kaye said so last night when she'd called? Nearly two hours of cleaning and straightening… Amanda shrugged. *Same old disapproving, resentful, competitive Kaye.* Maybe that was normal between sisters. *But it shouldn't be.*

By the time Kaye had used the bathroom and emerged with her nose wrinkled, only about twenty minutes had elapsed since her arrival. It was their longest visit in

Amanda couldn't remember how long.

Amanda watched her depart. Kaye's home metropolis was much larger and finer—better stores, more culture, and supposedly fewer hicks. But Amanda would rather live with hicks than pretentious snobs. Besides, small town friendliness—underrated by most big city dwellers—was dependable and comforting.

"So Kaye is too refined to stay here overnight." *Fine.* Kaye's presence would have complicated the newly-launched crisis management effort... in case Jason the creep *was* playing around. Amanda inhaled deeply and put on her game face—she had a dinner date with Jason the cheater.

2

What to talk about?

The country-casual restaurant bustled around their table. Without looking up, Amanda toyed with the gravy-soused noodles on her plate. Jason seemed different, and not merely because of Christine's shocking announcement. He was definitely acting funny, like he wished he were somewhere else. *Or would he rather be WITH someone else?* He seemed, well... guilty. Antsy and guilty.

Usually he talked about his current team or sports in general, but tonight he was mostly silent. *Guilty people either chatter non-stop... or they don't speak at all.*

Uncertain what to say, Amanda defaulted to shop-talk. "Louis dumped a new assignment on me today."

Jason looked up but continued chewing. His features had not actually *changed* in the past two days, yet they seemed different. He looked like a cheater.

"I don't have particulars yet, but it's his pet department that miraculously gets a grant almost every cycle. Somebody in Public Works has completely dropped the ball on their evaluations and King Louie's screaming bloody murder." Her boss typically assumed the worst, rarely made any legitimate queries, and went off half-cocked without any real investigation whatsoever. "I hate people who jump straight to the battle stations klaxon at the first radar blip." Most of

Amanda's military imagery came from war movies she'd watched with her father as a child. It had been one of her few refuges from domineering Kaye.

Jason just nodded and swallowed at the same time. *Awkward.* He'd been so uncomplicated and lovable... before this evening. But all of her high hopes for their future now seemed as limp and extraneous as the gristle he'd briskly trimmed off his roast beef slab.

Amanda nibbled on beef tips and sipped her iced tea before continuing. "Plus somehow or other Louis makes that my fault." Her job was reviewing and assessing applications from every Greene County agency seeking federal money. She was also responsible for collecting external evaluations at the end of the grant period, but she'd had no part in conducting them until now. "He wants me personally involved in their evals so this gets cleaned up quickly."

Jason didn't appear interested in anything except his buffet platter, but he'd repeatedly established eye contact as he ate. His blue eyes were at times bright with zeal but occasionally dark and soulful. They glazed slightly when Amanda talked shop. "So Monday you get thrown into the shark tank and have to evaluate their lack of effectiveness in spending Uncle Sam's money?" He scooted back his chair and stood.

She was surprised by Jason's perceptive feedback. "Tuesday, actually. We're closed Monday for Memorial..." Amanda broke off when Jason grabbed his plate and headed back to the buffet. *That was rude...* leaving in the middle of her reply! When had he started acting like that? Did rudeness go along with cheating? She fumed while Jason grazed at the seafood section. Friday evening's unrestricted portions and a dollar off the regular price made the restaurant a huge draw for Jason, among hundreds of other buffet fanatics. While she understood that, Amanda preferred smaller places with candlelight and atmosphere.

Finally he returned to his seat with a full plate and two desserts. "We don't have to talk about your work problems. Ruins the digestion." Jason smiled but it seemed strained.

Usually Amanda could smile back, but not after Christine's allegations. If she didn't talk about her job, the only logical subjects were sister Kaye or cheater Jason.

"Is anything else bothering you?" He appeared to struggle for the right words. "You seem... tense."

Amanda wanted to ask outright if he was playing around, but she hadn't even heard Christine's so-called evidence. She also fought the urge to search his glove compartment for someone else's panties. "Well, that dang New Year's Eve photo keeps coming up."

Jason almost grinned, but stopped. "I know that bothers you, but it doesn't really show anything. I mean, yeah, the view is up your short skirt while you're on a ten-foot ladder, but you had, uh, skivvies on. And pantyhose, right? So that's more clothes than you'd have at the pool."

She didn't feel like explaining why it mattered that photos of her underpinnings were circulating as attachments in e-mails and Facebook postings. Any woman would understand. That picture made it even more frustrating to deal with all the county and city departments. Because of Amanda's attractiveness, the most cynical co-workers assumed she'd gotten her important position for reasons other than work ethic and ability. That unfortunate photo only reinforced such views. *Views—hmm.*

Jason could tell she was upset but didn't know why. On the scale of Amanda's usual body language, it was more than the grant problem and worse than being reminded of that embarrassing photo. And it wasn't just her boss, because Louis was always a bully. So whatever was eating her was something distinctly different—larger, deeper, and more sinister. But what? He couldn't imagine. It was obvious from her fixed stare at the ketchup bottle that Amanda had zoned out on him, so Jason continued his meal.

In the middle of his chewing, Amanda suddenly resumed. "Oh, my sister finally told me why she and Tom are getting divorced."

He listened with only half an ear to this topical detour.

"Turns out Tommy-boy was *cheating* on her." It was weird, the way she stared at his face... like she was searching for a blemish.

Jason checked his watch. "Guess I have time for another quick dessert or two." Despite being often reminded of his predilection for beer, breaded and pan-fried meats, junk food, and frequent snacks, he was still fast and agile on the ball fields, with commendable endurance.

Amanda exhaled considerable air with extra sound. "I'm going to the powder room." She rose abruptly and stalked away.

Jason watched her leave—sexy view even when she was angry. Why would Kaye's divorce news bother Amanda? Normally she seemed secretly pleased when her elder sibling suffered any indignity.

Oh, well. He had his own fish to fry (besides what he'd

consumed at the buffet). The softball season schedule was screwing with his work shifts, their team "manager" couldn't coach his way through Little League practice, and not enough players were available for the big holiday tournament that coming weekend. Jason let a mouthful of artificial ice cream dissolve slightly before he swallowed. Plus, his fantasy league needed a baseball commissioner and so far nobody had volunteered to handle it. During supper he hadn't even wanted to think about his consultant problems at Greene County Electric Co-op. (The power company was known mainly by its initials, GCEC, which everyone pronounced Gee-keck.)

On top of everything else awry in Jason-Land, his friend Kevin Haywood had been regaling him with torrid tales of frequent alley-catting. It was bothersome that Kevin would try to bed a different woman nearly every night, but it worried Jason even more that he was vicariously titillated by the details. In fact, it made him feel a little guilty.

Amanda emerged from the restroom and lingered near the buffet's multiple desserts. She was strongly tempted, but managed to refrain by lacing her fingers together in front of her trim waist.

How could Jason be so insensitive? Couldn't he tell she was confused, worried, and furious? Didn't he *sense* that she'd been alerted to his indiscretion and was supremely ticked? How could he wolf down the equivalent of two complete meals while she felt like skinning him alive?

As she resumed her seat, she said, "You sure seem antsy tonight."

He appeared surprised that she'd noticed. "It's the MLB fantasy league draft at Roger Hardeman's apartment. If I get there late, Roger will mangle my picks in the first few rounds."

"Oh, I see," she replied. As an avid competitor in basketball, softball, soccer, and flag football, Jason sometimes seemed to value sports more than their relationship.

"Where is your sister, anyway? I'd thought she might join us."

Amanda eyed him suspiciously. Jason didn't do all that much thinking and when he did, it made him look guilty. "Oh, Kaye doesn't eat at these buffets... thinks they're too common. Plus she was huffy about staying in my guest-room. Evidently has a thing about boxes. Didn't say where she went, but most likely the same place as the company's meetings and exhibits. Probably downtown Nashville."

The evening had not gone well. Jason looked troubled and guilty of something, and she was pretty sure what it was.

She waited while he wiped his mouth with two napkins. While he paid the bill, she crossed her arms tightly and gazed through the window at the parking lot. Outside, Jason neglected to open his truck's passenger door for her. *Another slight! Taking up with floozies AND being rude!*

The short drive was silent and chilly despite the warm May evening. When they reached Amanda's duplex, Jason only said, "Late for the fantasy draft..." with a lame shrug. He actually moved toward her as if for a kiss, but Amanda stiffened and leaned away. She did not want any cheating lips on her face!

After he drove away, Amanda shut her apartment door

and slumped into the nearest chair. Too much strain from too many sources... she needed some relief. She reached up and banged on the front wall a few times. It would have been more satisfying to pound the wall she shared with her new neighbor, the yodeling one, but Amanda was too exhausted to get up.

She couldn't stop thinking about it. Jason, a cheater? Most of their time together had been nice... some had been excellent. But in truth, some aspects were quite unsatisfactory. Sex was still good, but there wasn't much measurable *romance*. Amanda had chalked this deficit to Jason's lack of sophistication. If he'd had more enlightening life experiences than commuting to Tennessee State University in West Nashville, she assumed he would automatically be more romantic. But maybe there were other reasons.

Her eyes half-closed, Amanda thought farther back, over those previous months they'd dated, off and on, nonexclusively. Jason had not been easy to catch. Lots of unattached women flocked around the team sports fields. It had been tricky to maneuver herself into his path and she'd had to elbow several others out of the way. Fortunately, Southern girls developed sharp elbows at an early age. It had been quite a competition to become Jason's girlfriend and Amanda had approached that challenge as vigorously as she had all her other obstacles in life.

Obstacles. A friend had phoned that morning and recited Amanda's Aries horoscope. What was it? She'd transcribed it word for word because it had seemed so important to kooky Sunny Cannon. These were not the normal few lines seen in most newspapers—it was a full-scale "horoscopic work-up" from Sunny's in-depth website search.

Where were those notes? Purse? No, briefcase. First flap

inside the lid. *Uhh*. Two distinct sections:

> *Look deeply into your relationship… it's a good time for you to pick up a few new clues from your sweetie. Deeply explore your moods, because you're in a really good position to make a seriously positive change. Be more willing to get rid of what you don't need.*
>
> *A big decision today, but the more you think about it, the murkier it gets. Really pore over the details of a big project to see if they all add up. Just let your intuition make the call. Once you're settled, it's time to move out quickly. Step up and enlist the aid of those who are sympathetic to your cause. Your emotions are leading you in a good direction, so even if things get weird, you need to press on righteously.*

It was typical mumbo jumbo to Amanda—vague but insinuated specificity. If all the horoscopes had been inadvertently scrambled by the website's layout crew, this one was general enough that any of the others might equally pertain to her. It could apply to work, finances, relatives, friendships—just about any aspect of life.

But this one mentioned relationships in the first sentence.

Thanks for reading! Dingbat Publishing strives to bring you quality entertainment that doesn't take itself too seriously. I mean honestly, with a name like that, our books have to be good or we're going to be laughed at. Or maybe both.

If you enjoyed this book, the best thing you can do is buy a million more copies and give them to all your friends… erm, leave a review on the readers' website of your preference. All authors love feedback and we take reviews from readers like you seriously.

Oh, and c'mon over to our website:
www.DingbatPublishing.Weebly.com

Who knows what other books you'll find there?

Cheers,

Gunnar Grey,
publisher, author, and Chief Dingbat